"I'm okay," Glynnis said.

She didn't look okay. She looked like hell. Tired, pale, and worried. Despite this, she looked younger than she had the day before, beautiful in no makeup, her hair tied back in a ponytail.

"I'm just so scared," she said.

"I know you are," Dan said. "That's one of the reasons I came by—to tell you that it may take a while, but we'll find your daughter."

Impulsively he got up and walked over to where she sat. Reaching down, he took her hand and pulled her to her feet. Then he did something he knew he shouldn't. He put his arms around Glynnis and held her while she cried.

Holding her trembling body, Dan silently repeated his pledge. He would find this woman's daughter and bring her safely home…if it was the last thing he ever did.

D0018191

Dear Reader,

Well, the lazy days of summer are winding to an end, so what better way to celebrate those last long beach afternoons than with a good book? We here at Silhouette Special Edition are always happy to oblige! We begin with *Diamonds and Deceptions* by Marie Ferrarella, the next in our continuity series, THE PARKS EMPIRE. When a mesmerizing man walks into her father's bookstore, sheltered Brooke Moss believes he's her dream come true. But he's about to challenge everything she thought she knew about her own family.

Victoria Pade continues her NORTHBRIDGE NUPTIALS with *Wedding Willies,* in which a runaway bride with an aversion to both small towns and matrimony finds herself falling for both, along with Northbridge's most eligible bachelor! In Patricia Kay's *Man of the Hour,* a woman finds her gratitude to the detective who found her missing child turning quickly to…love. In *Charlie's Angels* by Cheryl St. John, a single father is stymied when his little girl is convinced that finding a new mommy is as simple as having an angel sprinkle him with her "miracle dust"— until he meets the beautiful blonde who drives a rig called "Silver Angel." In *It Takes Three* by Teresa Southwick, a pregnant caterer sets her sights on the handsome single dad who swears his fatherhood days are behind him. Sure they are! And the MEN OF THE CHEROKEE ROSE series by Janis Reams Hudson concludes with *The Cowboy on Her Trail,* in which one night of passion with the man she's always wanted results in a baby on the way. Can marriage be far behind?

Enjoy all six of these wonderful novels, and please do come back next month for six more new selections, only from Silhouette Special Edition.

Gail Chasan
Senior Editor

Please address questions and book requests to:
Silhouette Reader Service
U.S.: 3010 Walden Ave., P.O. Box 1325, Buffalo, NY 14269
Canadian: P.O. Box 609, Fort Erie, Ont. L2A 5X3

Man of the Hour

PATRICIA KAY

Silhouette®

SPECIAL EDITION™

Published by Silhouette Books

America's Publisher of Contemporary Romance

This book is dedicated, with many thanks,
to Colleen Thompson—terrific writer,
knowledgeable reader and great friend.

 SILHOUETTE BOOKS

ISBN 0-373-24629-3

MAN OF THE HOUR

Copyright © 2004 by Patricia A. Kay

Visit Silhouette Books at www.eHarlequin.com

Printed in U.S.A.

Books by Patricia Kay

Silhouette Special Edition

*The Millionaire and
  the Mom* #1387
†*Just a Small-Town Girl* #1437
†*Annie and the Confirmed Bachelor* #1518
Secrets of a Small Town #1571
Man of the Hour #1629

Books previously published as Trisha Alexander

Silhouette Special Edition

Cinderella Girl #640
When Somebody Loves You #748
When Somebody Needs You #784
Mother of the Groom #801
When Somebody Wants You #822
Here Comes the Groom #845
Say You Love Me #875
What Will the Children Think? #906
Let's Make It Legal #924
The Real Elizabeth Hollister... #940
The Girl Next Door #965
This Child Is Mine #989
*A Bride for Luke #1024
*A Bride for John #1047
**A Baby for Rebecca* #1070
Stop the Wedding! #1097
Substitute Bride #1115
With This Wedding Ring #1169
A Mother for Jeffrey #1211
†*Wedding Bells and Mistletoe* #1289

†Callahans & Kin
*Three Brides and a Baby

PATRICIA KAY,

formerly writing as Trisha Alexander, is the *USA TODAY*
bestselling author of more that thirty contemporary
romances. She lives in Houston, Texas. To learn more
about her, visit her Web site at www.patriciakay.com.

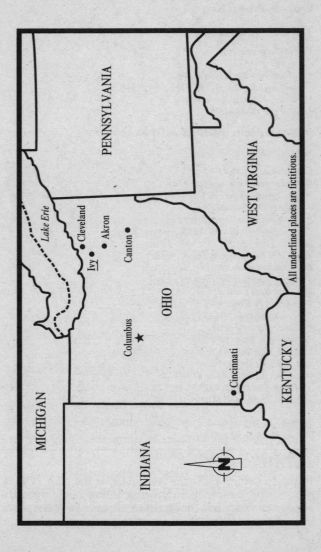

Chapter One

"Mommy, I thirsty!"

"Me, too! I wanna go home."

Glynnis March glanced down at her tired children. Michael, her seven-year-old, and Olivia, her three-year-old, looked mutinous.

"I'm sorry," she said as patiently as she could, considering the fact her head was pounding and all she wanted to do was to go home, too. "I know you're both tired. Five more minutes, okay? Mommy just needs to buy one more Christmas present, then we'll go to the food court."

"And get french fries?" Michael said.

Normally, Glynnis didn't allow the children to eat fast food, but desperate times called for desperate measures. "Yes, french fries and a soft drink you can take to the car and have while we're driving home, all right?"

Michael, skeptical, frowned. "You promise?"

"I promise."

With an expression that pierced her because it was one she'd seen on his father's face many times, Michael looked down at his sister and said, "Just five minutes, Livvy. Mommy promised."

"Fibe minutes?" Olivia frowned in concentration, putting out four fingers one by one.

Glynnis couldn't help it; she chuckled and pulled out Olivia's thumb. "Five, honey. One, two, three, four, five."

Olivia counted along with her mother and then grinned, her dimples deep and adorable. "Fibe."

Michael didn't smile. He was too old to be distracted. Glynnis knew she was pushing her luck. But Corinne's Closet had cashmere sweaters at half price—something she hadn't known until she'd seen the sign in the window—and she knew if she didn't go in and get one now, they'd be gone by the time she was able to come back to the mall. And a green cashmere sweater would be the perfect gift for her sister-in-law, Sabrina.

Praying the children would last long enough for her to snag the sweater, Glynnis—children in tow—entered the shop. She nearly turned around and walked out when she saw how many women were ahead of her. It was a mob scene. But she wanted that sweater for Sabrina.

Maneuvering through the crowd, she spied the sweater section. It wasn't easy, but she managed to work her way to the table where the sale sweaters were stacked. Oh, good, she thought, seeing that there were several different shades of green. She especially liked the mossy shade, which would be a perfect complement to Sabrina's eyes.

"Glynnis! Fancy seeing you here."

Glynnis whirled at the sound of the Scottish accent. As she'd thought, Isabel McNabb, head of the creative writing program at Ivy Community College, where Glynnis taught art and art history, stood grinning at her.

"Hi, Isabel. Yeah, I'm braving the madding crowd."

"Isn't it *just*." Isabel pushed back a strand of wayward blond hair. "But my mum is coming tomorrow, and I still haven't bought anything for her. So here I am."

"Mom*my!* Come *on!*" Michael tugged his hand away from Glynnis's grip.

Glynnis looked down at her unhappy son. His dark eyes, another reminder of his father, were accusatory. "Honey," she began.

"I wanna go. You *promised.*"

"You pomised," Olivia echoed, her tongue not able to navigate her *R*s very well. She, too, started trying to release herself.

Glynnis hefted Olivia into her arms. "Isabel, I'm sorry. I can't talk. I've got to get one of those sweaters and get out of here or my kids are going to have a meltdown."

Isabel nodded. Lowering her voice, she said, "See why I have no desire for the little darlings?"

Glynnis grinned. Isabel's dry humor and fearlessness about expressing an unpopular opinion never failed to amuse her. "Have a wonderful Christmas," she said as Isabel waved goodbye.

"You, too."

Turning to the table with the sweaters, Glynnis began a one-handed search for a mossy-green one in a size small. Olivia, held in the other arm, began sucking her thumb. On another day, Glynnis would have tried to distract her and gently pull the thumb out of her mouth, but right now she was too frazzled. If the thumb gave Livvy some comfort and allowed Glynnis to get her sweater and get out of there quickly, so be it. She'd deal with her daughter's insecurities some other time.

Just when Glynnis found the size she was looking for, there was a huge crash as one of the nearby circular racks holding leather jackets collapsed onto the floor. Glancing over, she spied the unmistakable red sneakers of her son protruding from underneath the fallen rack.

"Michael!" Putting Olivia down, Glynnis rushed over to help one of the sales clerks right the rack. A dazed-looking Michael stared up at her. There was a bloody cut on his cheek. "Oh, Michael, honey," Glynnis said, reaching down to help him up. "Are you okay?"

"Uh-huh."

Glynnis took a deep breath. Her heart was racing.

She gathered Michael into a hug. "I'm so sorry," she said to the clerk.

The sales clerk just rolled her eyes. "Hey, he's a kid. We're used to it."

Glynnis smiled thankfully. Reaching into her pocket, she extracted a tissue and gently wiped away the blood from Michael's cheek. Grateful to see the injury was only a surface scratch, she mentally dismissed the green sweater and said, "C'mon, honey, let's go."

"Okay," he said.

"Livvy, sweetie, we're going home." Glynnis turned, then frowned as she realized Olivia wasn't behind her. Remembering that she'd put Olivia down when the rack fell, she called out, "Livvy? Livvy, honey, where are you?" She made a quick sweep of the store, but she didn't see her daughter or the bright yellow jacket she was wearing anywhere. "Livvy!" she called louder, the first small seeds of panic beginning to take hold. "Stop hiding. This isn't funny."

"What is it?" the clerk who'd helped her with Michael said.

"My little girl. I can't see her. She…oh, God." Fear caused her voice to shake. "I—I had her in my arms, and I put her down when I saw Michael under the rack." Glynnis was practically crying now. "She's gone! I don't see her anywhere."

Holding on to Michael tightly, Glynnis raced through the store. Livvy had to be here somewhere! Maybe she was hiding under one of the racks. The kids loved to do that. Once, Michael had scared her half to death by hiding and not answering when she called. When she'd finally found him, he giggled, completely unaware of the fact he'd taken a few years off her life expectancy.

By now, many of the customers and all the clerks realized what had happened and they were clustered in worried-looking groups.

"Ma'am, ma'am, slow down. Tell me what your daughter looks like," the clerk said.

"She…she's only three. Th-three and a half. She's small with reddish-gold hair like mine, hazel eyes, dimples, sh-she's wearing a bright yellow down jacket with a hood. Um, navy blue corduroy pants and white sneakers." Glynnis fought her fear, telling herself Olivia was tired, and she'd probably just curled up somewhere.

"Anything else, ma'am?"

"Sh-she was sucking her thumb." The mention of the thumb caused something inside Glynnis to splinter. "She's probably just hiding somewhere." *Please, God, let her just be playing hide-and-seek.*

"I'll get security," the clerk said. Calling to a co-worker, she added, "Help her look."

The other clerk organized the staff and remaining customers, all of whom seemed to have stopped whatever they'd been doing to commiserate. Systematically, they began searching under and behind racks and counters.

Soon they'd exhausted all possibilities, and Livvy was nowhere to be seen.

Glynnis, holding on to Michael as if her life depended upon it, raced to the door and out into the mall. Her gaze darted around. *Livvy, Livvy, Livvy, where are you?* But no matter how hard she looked, she saw no yellow jacket. She saw no Olivia. Biting her lip to keep from crying, Glynnis stood numbly. She had never felt so helpless in her life.

"Mommy? Where's Livvy?" Michael's voice trembled.

Looking down into his worried eyes, Glynnis could see he was on the verge of tears. She tried to make her own voice reassuring. "We'll find her, honey. Don't worry. We'll find her. M-maybe she just wanted to get some french fries." But even as Glynnis said the words, the fear she'd been trying to keep tamped down erupted, threatening to totally overwhelm her.

A few seconds later, two black-uniformed security guards—one an older man, the other, a plump young woman—converged on the store.

The sales clerk who had been so helpful took Glynnis by the arm. "Come back inside," she said. "We've got a security camera. Let's look at the tape and see if your daughter wandered outside."

"What happened, ma'am?" the female guard said.

By now, Glynnis was so panicked, she could hardly talk, so the clerk hastily filled in. As soon as the vital information was imparted, the male guard got out his walkie-talkie. Within minutes, the background music that was so much a part of the mall went silent and the public address system blared into life.

"Don't worry, ma'am," the male guard said. "We're closing off every exit. If your little girl wandered off by herself, she won't be able to get out. We'll find her."

"Lucy," called one of the clerks.

The clerk, who had been so helpful from the beginning, turned.

"We've got the security tape rewound."

"Let's go look at that tape, ma'am," the female guard said.

In the store's office, Glynnis, with Michael, the store manager, the two guards and Lucy, the helpful clerk, stood and watched the security tape.

"Oh, God!" Glynnis gasped. "There! There! That's her!" She began to cry, for there, on the now-stopped tape, was Olivia. But she wasn't wandering out the door alone. She was being held in the arms of a young woman, and she was crying. "That woman is taking my baby!"

The male guard grabbed the phone and punched in some numbers. "I'm calling the police," he said. Inclining his head toward the female guard, he said, "Alert everyone. Be on the lookout for a female, teens or twenties, wearing a short jacket and jeans, spiked hairdo, probably streaked blond, carrying a female youngster. Give them a description of Mrs. March's little girl. Tell them not to try to apprehend, just to watch and follow. The doors are all locked now, so she can't leave. Call me the minute you see them."

His eyes met Glynnis's and, unknowingly, he parroted almost the exact words she'd used to reassure Michael. "We'll find her, ma'am. Don't worry. We'll find her."

Please God, Glynnis prayed, *please let him be right. Please let them find her. Don't let her be hurt. Just bring her back to me, and I'll never ask you for anything again.*

Dan O'Neill's shift began at three, but he'd been bored at home and decided to come in to the station early. Although you'd think the opposite would be true—that perps would take a break during the Christmas holidays—crime seemed to increase at this time of year.

Even Ivy, Ohio, with its population of less than 35,000, wasn't immune. Of course, instead of nonstop homicides, drug deals gone bad and armed robbery—which had been the menu in Chicago—the majority of crime in Ivy was confined to domestic disputes and vandalism, with a few drunk drivers thrown in.

Not exactly exciting, he thought wryly.

But then he hadn't moved to Ivy for excitement. In his years with the Chicago PD, he'd had enough excitement to last him a lifetime.

Remembering Chicago and the reasons behind his leaving, he felt a familiar mantle of depression settling onto his shoulders. Quickly, before it could gain a firm hold, he shook it off. He was tired of feeling bad. Tired of feeling guilty. Tired of the old Dan.

Soon it would be a new year.

A new year.

He repeated the phrase mentally several times. New years meant changes. Resolutions. Getting rid of bad habits and adopting new ones.

"It's a new life," he muttered.

"You say something?"

Dan looked up. Romeo Navarro, aptly named because he considered himself God's gift to women, was looking at him curiously.

"Just talking to myself," Dan said.

"Gotta watch that. That's what old people do."

Dan shrugged.

Romeo started to say something else when the phone rang. Both men turned to look at Elena, the dispatcher. "Oh, that's awful!" she said, her dark eyes getting big as she listened. "Someone will be right there." She disconnected the call and then knocked on the glass window of the chief's office. "Chief Crandall!"

Gabe Crandall—short, bald, paunchy, and counting the months until retirement—looked up.

"A little kid disappeared from one of the stores at the mall," Elena said.

Dan and Romeo were on their feet before Chief Crandall barked out their names. Dan reached for his suit coat. Putting it on, he checked to make sure it didn't catch on his .40 caliber Glock, holstered on his belt. The change from a shoulder holster was a welcome one, although he knew some police departments were still debating its merits, mainly because old-timers were resistant to any kind of change, no matter how much proof there was that a cop's range of motion was too limited with the shoulder holster.

By the time Dan had put on his overcoat, Romeo was ready.

Chief Crandall stood in the doorway of his office. "O'Neill, you're in charge."

Dan nodded. He wondered what Romeo was thinking. Until Dan joined the department three months earlier, Romeo had been the senior officer on the force.

"You need more backup, call Elena. She'll round up everyone she can find," the chief added.

Elena gave them the particulars and five minutes later they were on their way in a department Malibu, with Romeo driving. As they sped toward the mall, which was located on the west side of town, they went over the meager information they'd been provided.

The victim was a three-year-old girl. She'd been picked up and carried off by an unknown woman. Dan swore under his breath.

Three years old.

Luckily, the snatch had been caught on the store's security tape. Maybe they'd keep being lucky. Maybe by the time they reached the mall, the little girl would be found, and there'd be nothing for him and Romeo to do but go back to the station. Holding on to that thought, he tried to not to think about the alternative.

When they arrived at the Ivy Mall, Dan was glad to see the outside doors had been secured. He just hoped they'd been secured in time.

He and Romeo showed their badges, and a tall, dark-haired civilian unlocked the doors to let them in.

"I'm Jack Robertson," he said, "the mall manager." His gray eyes behind wire-rimmed glasses reflected his concern. "Thanks for getting here so fast."

Dan and Romeo introduced themselves and then followed Robertson through the crowded mall to a spot near the center, where the mall's Santa was enthroned. Dan didn't have to be told that the shop labeled Corinne's Closet was the scene of the snatch, not just because there were so many people congregated outside the store, but because the air fairly hummed with excitement. The tension was a dead giveaway that here was the unusual, here something had happened that was outside the norm.

Inside, the crowd parted, and he and Romeo were taken to the back of the store where there was a small office. Dan immediately knew the pretty redhead seated in the corner was the mother of the three-year-old. Her haunted eyes and strained, pale face told the whole story. Standing beside her was a small, dark-haired boy who looked tired and frightened.

Dan nodded to the woman, and their eyes met briefly. He could feel the weight of her fear. He wished he could tell her there was no reason to worry, but experience had taught him the opposite.

Also crowded into the office was a middle-aged male security guard with a name tag that read Harold Fury, and two women who wore name tags identifying them as store personnel.

Dan held out his hand to the security guard. "Lieutenant Dan O'Neill. Ivy Police Department."

Romeo stepped forward. "Sergeant Romeo Navarro."

The security guard introduced himself, then gestured toward the woman. "This here is Mrs. March, the missing child's mother."

Dan looked at the mother again. "We'll talk in a minute."

She bit her lip and drew the boy—Dan imagined it was her son—closer to her.

Addressing the guard again, Dan said, "I understand there's a security tape."

"Yes."

"May we see it, please?"

When the tape reached the point where it showed the abduction, Dan asked that the tape be stopped so he could study the woman. She was distinctive, even though they couldn't see her face. That punk hairdo alone would make her stand out in a crowd.

"Did anyone see this woman in the store?" he asked.

"I did," said the younger-looking clerk, a pretty blonde.

Dan glanced at her name tag. "Tell me what you saw, Lucy."

"I only saw her briefly. She was at the counter in the front where we have a display of turquoise jewelry. I was going to go ask if I could help her, but another customer asked me a question and I forgot about her."

"Was there anything unusual about her? Other than her hair?"

"I'm sorry. I just didn't notice anything in particular. She was young, in her teens or early twenties, maybe, that's about all I remember. And her jacket was black. I did notice that. Black leather. It was nice. Oh, and I think she had on blue jeans."

Dan smiled. "Good. That's good. Most people remember more than they think."

The girl smiled, obviously proud of herself.

"Has the entire mall been secured?" Dan asked the guard.

"Yes. All the outside doors are locked."

"In all the stores?"

"Yes."

"You checked them all?" Dan said dubiously.

"No, but the order went out." For the first time, the guard showed hesitation. "Everyone was told to lock their doors."

"How many security people do you have on duty?"

"Four, counting me."

"And how many stores are in this mall?"

"Thirty-five."

"Including the big anchor stores?"

"Yes."

Dan realized they would need all the police and security personnel they could round up if they were going to conduct the kind of search that needed to be conducted.

While Romeo and the security guard called for backup, Dan turned his attention to the mother.

"Mrs. March, I want to assure you that we'll do everything in our power to find your little girl."

She swallowed. "Thank you."

"Do you have a picture of her?"

"Yes, yes, I do." Reaching down, she picked up a handbag from the floor and opened it. A moment later, she held out a photograph. Her hand was trembling.

Dan knew there was no place for emotion during an investigation. The mother's naked fear and silent plea for him to accomplish a miracle was bad enough. But the sight of the beautiful child in the photo was the ultimate test of his ability to stay objective and professional. She was a real cutie, with a dimpled smile, laughing hazel eyes and curly red-gold hair the same shade as her mother's.

Although he fought them, he couldn't stop the memories as the image of another beautiful little girl assaulted him. Pain, as fresh as if the death of his beloved daughter had taken place yesterday instead of nine years ago, punched him in the gut.

For a moment, he stood paralyzed. Then from somewhere he found the strength to push those agonizing memories away so he could concentrate all of his attention and skill on finding this child.

"May I keep this picture?" His voice was more brusque than he'd intended. Softening it, he added, "In case we need it."

"Y-yes, of course."

"I just have a few more questions."

"All right."

"Is there any chance someone you know could be behind this abduction?"

Her eyes widened in disbelief. "Someone I *know?* No one I know would *ever* do anything like this."

"There's no ex-husband? Nobody who might wish you harm?"

Her look of outrage faded. She shook her head. "No. I—I'm a...widow."

"I'm sorry. Look, finding your daughter might take a while. Is there anyone you can call to come and be here with you?"

"I...yes. My brother." The relief on her face was palpable. She dug a cell phone out of her handbag.

While she placed her phone call, Dan walked over to see how Romeo and the security guard had fared.

"Elena rounded up all ten patrolmen," Romeo said, "as well as DeChurch, Nichols, Richardson and

Cavelli." The last four were the other detectives in the department.

"And I've called in as many of our security guards as I could find," the guard said.

"Which is how many?" Dan asked.

"Six."

Dan thought fast. "Okay. Here's what we'll do. We'll divide up the anchor stores first. All customers and clerks will be asked to leave by one of the outside doors where one patrolman and one guard will be stationed. Everyone's ID will be checked before they're allowed to leave, and everyone will be quizzed about whether they might have seen the woman and child. Anyone with a small child will get extra attention. While this is proceeding, a team will start on the second floor of each store and systematically search each area. After each area is searched, we'll cordon if off and put a security guard there to make sure no one tries to go back into that particular area to hide."

"This might take more manpower than we've got," Romeo said in an aside.

Ignoring the remark—which was true, but unproductive—Dan went on to say that all the people in the other stores or in the public areas would be asked to leave from the north entrance, where two police officers would check each person's identification.

"Sergeant Navarro will be in charge of the north entrance, which is also where we'll admit anyone who's coming to help." Turning to the mall manager,

Dan said, "Can we use your office as our command post?"

"Of course."

"Okay. Romeo, send all additional help there."

"What do you want me to do?" This question came from Harold Fury.

"Mr. Fury, you round up all your security guards and bring them to the management office, too. I'll brief them and give them their individual assignments."

Once Romeo and Fury were dispatched, he looked over at the mother. She was no longer on the phone. "Is someone coming?" he asked her.

She nodded. "My best friend. I—I couldn't find my brother."

"Okay, good. I'm glad you'll have someone to stay with you." He tried to make his smile reassuring. "I want you to stay here for the time being, okay?"

"All right. You…" She took a deep breath. "You're going to find her, aren't you?"

He hesitated, torn between the brutal truth and something else, something that would give this woman the strength to endure. He nodded grimly. "Yes. We're going to find her."

Seeing the blind trust in her eyes, he vowed he would keep his promise if it was the last thing he ever did.

Chapter Two

Glynnis sat in stunned silence.

She wasn't sure how much time had passed since that detective left, but it seemed like hours. She couldn't remember his name, either. All she knew was that he had kind eyes, and they made her want to believe him when he said they'd find Olivia.

Please, God, she prayed over and over again. *Please let them find her, and let her be okay. Please.*

She kept seeing the way Livvy's face had looked in the video, all crumpled and scared. By now, she must be terrified. Glynnis bit her lip and clenched her hands to keep them from shaking uncontrollably.

My baby.

How could she have put Livvy down without grabbing on to her hand? Making sure something like this couldn't happen? What kind of mother was she, anyway? *All my life I've been making terrible choices. What is* wrong *with me?*

Although she knew it did no good to dwell on the past, she couldn't seem to stop herself today. Was God punishing her for her bad judgment? For all the mistakes she'd made, especially the worst one nineteen years ago? Was he telling her to be more careful in the future?

Glynnis jumped up and began to pace around the store.

Gregg, where are you? I need you...

In all of her life, her brother was the only one she'd ever been able to depend upon. Everyone else had let her down, but Gregg never had.

They'd always been close, and after their parents died when they were sixteen, they'd become even closer.

But she hadn't been able to find Gregg today. There was no answer at the house, he wasn't at the restaurant and when she tried his cell phone, she got his voice mail. She'd left a message, then another with Janine, the hostess at Antonelli's, the restaurant Gregg had owned for the past six years.

Poor Janine. She'd been so upset. She'd kept apologizing and saying she wasn't sure where Gregg had gone, only that he'd left at noon and said he wouldn't be back today.

"If he calls, I'll be sure and tell him what happened. Do you have your cell phone with you? Is there anything anyone else can do? Do you want Steve to come?"

Steve was Glynnis's and Gregg's cousin, and for nearly two years he'd been Gregg's right-hand man at the restaurant.

"No," Glynnis said, "that's okay. You need him there."

"What about Kat? I could call her for you."

Kat Sherman was Glynnis's best friend, and everyone at the restaurant knew her.

"Thanks. I—I'll call her myself."

Kat hadn't let her down. "You just hold on," she said when Glynnis told her what had happened. "I'll be there in thirty minutes."

That had been twenty-five minutes ago, so Kat should arrive at any time.

"Mommy?"

Startled, Glynnis blinked.

"Mommy, I have to go to the bathroom."

"Oh, honey, I'm sorry." What was wrong with her? She'd almost forgotten her son was there, he'd been so quiet. "There's a bathroom right there." She turned and pointed to the door behind them.

"Okay."

"Do I need to come with you?"

Michael shook his head. "Nuh-uh."

"Be sure to wash your hands when you're done."

"I know."

She watched him as he walked inside. He was such a good kid. So was Livvy. They were wonderful children. They were the reason she could never regret her relationship with their father, for if she hadn't married Ben March, she wouldn't have had Michael and Olivia. They were worth any amount of humiliation she had suffered over her gullibility and misplaced trust in their father.

When Michael came out of the bathroom, he said, "Mom, where did Livvy go?"

The look in his eyes almost broke her heart, and she drew him into a hug. The feel of his warm body, the trusting way he wrapped his arms around her neck, was nearly her undoing. "I don't know, honey, but I don't want you to worry. The policemen will find her."

"But *why* did she go? She knows she's not s'posed to go anywhere with strangers!"

"Oh, honey, I—" What could she say that wouldn't frighten him?

"Glynnis?"

"Aunt Kat!" Forgetting all about his question, Michael broke away from Glynnis and ran to Kat, who stood in the doorway of the small office. The children adored Kat, so much so that Glynnis had deemed her an honorary aunt. Kat bent down and gave Michael a hug. When she straightened, her eyes were suspiciously shiny.

Glynnis had never been so glad to see anyone in her life. She got up, and the two women hugged hard.

"Glynnis, this is just awful. I am *so* sorry."

Glynnis swallowed against the lump in her throat. "It's all my fault."

"Oh, hon, don't blame yourself. You can't watch them every second."

"Don't try to make me feel better, Kat. I'm a total screwup. I can't do anything right."

Kat took her by the shoulders. "Now you listen to me, Glynnis Antonelli." Fiercely loyal and outraged by Ben March's deceit and bigamous marriage to Glynnis, she never used the March name. In fact, Kat had tried to persuade Glynnis to change the children's names. Glynnis had considered it, but in the end, she'd decided it would only hurt and confuse them, especially Michael, who was old enough to question the reason.

"You are *not* a screwup," Kat continued vehemently. You've had some rotten breaks, that's all. None of what's happened has been your fault."

"I lost my child, Kat! What kind of mother loses her child? All for a sweater. For a stupid sweater! I knew they were tired and cranky, yet I had to push them. Why couldn't I have just taken them home when they wanted to go?" She could hear her voice rising and knew she was becoming hysterical, knew she was frightening Michael, yet she couldn't seem to stop. "Oh, Kat…" she cried.

"Ah, honey…"

This time when Kat put her arms around Glynnis, Glynnis broke down.

"Mommy?"

"Mom's okay," Kat assured Michael. Fiercely, she whispered in Glynnis's ear. "Get ahold of yourself. You're scaring Michael."

Drawing on every ounce of strength she possessed, Glynnis got herself under control again.

"Okay, now calmly tell me everything," Kat said. She put her arm around Michael and drew him close.

When Glynnis finished, Kat wore her determined look, the one that meant she was going to take charge. "What're the police doing? Besides checking people at the exit? Are they searching all the stores? Did they put out an Amber Alert? Contact the TV stations? Who's in charge? Do you know? Is my brother here?" The questions tumbled out in a rapid-fire barrage.

"I don't know who's in charge," Glynnis said. "I can't remember his name. I was in such a fog when he got here, I didn't hear what he said. He seemed to know what he was doing, though."

"I hope so. You do know my brother moved back and is now working for the Ivy Police Department, right? I told you, didn't I?"

"Yes." But until now, Glynnis had forgotten.

"Well, we need to get him out here if he's not here already. He's got all kinds of experience that these small-town cops don't have."

"For all I know, he might be here. The two officers who came initially sent for more backup."

"I'll call him just to make sure." Kat whipped out her cell phone and punched in a few numbers. She tapped her small, booted foot impatiently as she waited. "He's not home. I'll call the station."

Glynnis watched her. If she hadn't been so worried and frightened she might have been amused. Kat was never unsure of herself; she never hesitated. She saw a problem, she decided on a course of action and she jumped in with both feet. Glynnis wished she could be like that. Anytime *she'd* made a quick decision, it had turned out to be a bad mistake. Now caution was her watchword. *Except for today. Today you weren't cautious at all.*

"Uh-huh. Uh-huh. Oh, really?" Kat grinned at Glynnis and made an *O* with her thumb and forefinger. A few seconds later, she switched the phone off. "Dan *is* here. He's the detective in charge of the case."

"You're kidding." Glynnis pictured the detective who had been so kind—the dark, unruly hair, the world-weary blue eyes, the tall, athletic body. Now that she knew he was Kat's brother Dan, she immediately saw the resemblance. "He was so nice."

"Does he know who you are?" Kat asked. "And by the way, where is he?"

"I don't know. To both questions. He said he was setting up a command post in the management office, so he could be there."

"Is the management office down by the food court?"

"Yes, I think so. I'm sure I've seen a sign when I've used those rest rooms down there."

"Want to walk down and see if we can find him?"

"I don't think I should. He told me to stay here…just in case."

"In case what?"

"You know." Glynnis realized they'd already said too much in front of Michael, but what could she do? He was avidly listening. "In case Livvy should come back here looking for me."

"But…" Kat stopped at the expression on Glynnis's face. She glanced down at Michael. "Of course. That was silly of me. All right. I'll go down and see if Dan's at the management office and try to find out what I can. Want me to get you guys anything to eat or drink while I'm there?"

Glynnis looked at Michael. "Do you want something to eat from the food court, honey?"

He nodded. "Uh-huh."

"Yes, please," Glynnis corrected automatically.

"Yes, please," he echoed.

"What would you like?" Kat asked.

"Chicken nuggets and a Coke?" he said hopefully, eyeing Glynnis.

"Whatever you want," she said.

"Some french fries, too?" Kat said.

"Okay. And will you get me lots of ketchup?" He turned to Glynnis. "Mom, can we get some for Livvy, too? 'Cause when she comes back, she'll be hungry." The worried look was back in his eyes.

"Livvy will probably want to pick out her own food." It was all Glynnis could think to say.

"I know what she likes," he said stubbornly.

"Tell you what," Kat said. "Why don't you come with me, Michael? That way you can see everything they have and if you decide you want something else, you can get it. You can also tell Livvy everything they have, since she can't read yet."

Glynnis shot Kat a grateful look. "That's a good idea." She opened her handbag to get her wallet.

"Put that money away," Kat said in her I-won't-tolerate-any-argument voice. "What can I get you, Glynnis? Sandwich? Coffee? A Coke? A bottle of water?"

"Just coffee."

"You sure?"

"Yes, I'm sure."

"Okay. We'll be back. See you later." Kat took Michael's hand. "Let's go, slugger."

Glynnis followed them outside and watched as they walked away. The ache in her chest was so huge that it was hard to breathe. Michael looked so little and so vulnerable. Every instinct told her to run after them and snatch Michael back. She knew that was crazy. Nothing bad would happen to him in Kat's care. After all, Kat was not a screwup. *She'd* never lost a child.

Unlike you, who've now lost two.

The dark thought, which had been trying to surface for hours, slammed into Glynnis with the force of a hurricane.

Shaking, she stumbled back into the shop.

Dan was halfway back to Corinne's Closet when he saw his sister Kat and the March woman's little boy walking toward him.

"What are *you* doing here?" he said.

"Glynnis called me."

"Glynnis?"

"Have you met Michael, Dan? Michael, honey, this is my brother, Lieutenant O'Neill. And Dan, this is Michael. His mom is Glynnis Antonelli, my best friend. Michael, why don't you go look at the puppies?" There was a pet store a few feet away. "I'll just be a minute." To Dan she said, "It's okay if he goes over there, isn't it?"

If there had been people around, Dan would have said no. He sure didn't want another kid going missing. But all the pedestrian traffic had been cleared out of the inner part of the mall, so there was no danger to Michael. "Sure, it's okay." Dan would keep one eye on him anyway. Once Michael was out of earshot, Dan said, "I thought her name was March."

"She goes by March. See, she married this March guy and it turned out he was already married. A fact he conveniently didn't tell her. Which means they were never legally married at all." Kat's expression left no room for doubt about her feelings.

"Why do you call her Antonelli if she goes by March?"

"Because I refuse to acknowledge that bastard," Kat said with that look he knew well, the obstinate one that said she'd made up her mind and nothing anyone else said was going to make a bit of difference. Of all his siblings, Kat was the most unbending when she felt she was right.

"How's she doing?" he asked.

"She's hanging in there. More important, how are *you* doing?"

"The investigation's moving along. We're searching all the stores. If we find her here, great. In the meantime, we'll call in an Amber Alert, which will broadcast the details nationwide and alert all appropriate authorities."

"Do you think there's any chance the woman is still here somewhere?"

Dan shrugged. "That's impossible to know. I hope she is, but if she isn't, it'll be hours before we know for sure, because it's going to take time to do a complete search of all the stores. Hell, there are five anchor stores here. That alone is a massive job."

"Oh, Dan, you've *got* to find Olivia. You've just got to. Glynnis has already been through so much. If something has happened to Olivia, it…it would destroy her."

"Believe me, I want to find that child just as much as you do."

Just then, the boy walked back to them. "I'm hungry, Aunt Kat."

"I'm sorry, Michael." Turning back to Dan, she said, "I promised Michael some food. That's where we were headed."

"You go on. And after you get your food, you can take it to the management office. They've got a waiting room there that's a lot more comfortable than the little office at Corinne's Closet."

"But Glynnis is waiting for us at the store."

"I'm going there now. I'll get her and bring her to where you are."

"Okay. See you in a little while."

When Dan got to the store, he saw Glynnis March out front.

"I'm sorry," she said. "I couldn't stand sitting back in that office one minute longer."

Now that Dan knew more about her situation, he felt even worse for her. She was showing the strain of the past hour. It hurt to see the plea in her eyes, because he had no good news for her. "That's okay. I actually came back to tell you that I thought it would be okay for you to come to the management office now."

She looked stricken. "Oh."

"That doesn't mean you should give up hope. Or that we have. It only means that I don't think your little girl will be brought back here. Just to be sure, though, that guard—" he inclined his head in the direction of the security guard standing nearby "—will stay here, even after the store is locked up."

She nodded. "All right. Thank you."

"Wait for me here. I'll go in and tell the manager she can lock up."

When Dan came back outside, she said, "Kat told me you're her brother. When you introduced yourself, I was so frightened, I don't think I even heard your name."

He smiled. "It's Dan. Dan O'Neill."

"And I'm Glynnis, but you already knew that."

"I wish we could have met under happier circumstances."

"Me, too."

They walked the rest of the way in silence. Dan wondered what was going through her mind. He hoped she wasn't blaming herself, but he was afraid she was. He wanted to tell her that no matter how careful a parent was, things like this happened. He also wanted to tell her he understood how helpless she was feeling. But he knew neither would be a comfort to her, so he said nothing.

When they reached the management office, he ushered her inside, where Kat and the boy were already seated around the coffee table. The smell of french fries made Dan's stomach grumble, and he realized he hadn't eaten since breakfast. He glanced at his watch. Almost five-thirty. Soon everyone would be getting hungry and they would have to be fed. Dan had been prepared for this contingency and had asked several of the food venues to stay open for just that purpose. The men could eat in shifts; that way, the search could continue without interruption.

Dan left the women and the boy in the outer waiting area and walked back into the manager's office, which he'd commandeered for his own. It was time to call each of his men to get a progress report.

After that, he would decide if they needed to call in any neighboring law enforcement personnel to speed things along.

He picked up the phone.

* * *

At eight o'clock, when the search for Olivia had been going on for more than four hours with no good news, Gregg and Sabrina finally arrived at the mall.

Glynnis broke down when she saw them. "Thank God you're here." She tried not to cry, but one look at her brother's worried face and she couldn't hold back the tears.

"I'm sorry, Glynnie. We went to Columbus," Gregg said, folding her into his arms. "I wanted to meet with this possible new vendor and Sabrina wanted to finish up her shopping there."

"We were just sick when we heard what happened," Sabrina said.

"I'm just glad you're here now."

When she was calm, she filled them in on everything she hadn't been able to say in her message. Throughout, Sabrina held her hand.

Glynnis loved Sabrina. Their relationship had been awkward in the beginning, because Sabrina was Ben's daughter, and Glynnis hadn't found out about her existence until Ben had died.

In fact, Sabrina was the one who came to Ivy to break the news—something Ben had asked her to do in a letter he'd left with his lawyer. That was tough on her. Her mother, Isabel—Ben's only legal wife— was hysterical over Ben's double life and mortified by the scandal it had caused in their little town. She would have felt completely betrayed by Sabrina if she'd known of her daughter's involvement with her husband's other family.

Sabrina had been put in a horrible position, which only became more difficult as she got to know Glynnis and the children, whom she'd immediately loved.

And then, complicating matters even further, she fell in love with Gregg. For a while, no one who knew the story thought it could possibly have a happy ending, but it did. In fact, Gregg and Sabrina were one of the happiest couples Glynnis had ever known. And not long ago, their happiness had become complete when, on their daughter Samantha's christening day, Sabrina's mother had forgiven Sabrina and the two had reconciled.

Isabel was remarried now, which was a whole other story.

Thinking back over the rocky road they'd all traveled, Glynnis knew they were lucky to have ended up a loving family unit. Glynnis would have loved Sabrina under any circumstances, simply because she made Gregg so happy. It was a bonus that she was such a wonderful person and someone Glynnis would have enjoyed having as a friend even if they hadn't been related.

When Glynnis finished explaining everything, Gregg said he'd like to talk to the cop in charge.

"That's the other thing I wanted to tell you," Glynnis said. "He's Kat's brother."

Gregg turned to Kat. "I didn't know you had a brother on the police force."

"Dan's six years older than me and he's lived in Chicago since he was twenty. He was with the Chicago PD for more than seventeen years. Three months ago he decided he needed a change, so he moved back to Ivy, and now he's a lieutenant with the Ivy Police Department."

"That's good news," Gregg said. "He's probably got a lot more experience than most of the cops on the force."

"Yes," Kat said. "He does. And believe me, he'll do everything possible to find Olivia. Everything."

"I'd still like to talk to him."

"Then let's go see if we can find him," Kat said.

"I'll stay here with Glynnis and Michael," Sabrina said. She smiled down at Michael, who hadn't left her side since she'd arrived.

After Kat and Gregg left them, Sabrina said, "Are you doing okay? Is there anything I can get you? Something to eat?"

Glynnis shook her head. The thought of food made her feel sick.

"What about you, Michael?" Sabrina said.

"He ate earlier," Glynnis said.

"A cookie, maybe?"

Glynnis knew Sabrina just needed to feel she was doing something useful, even if it was only feeding them. God knows Glynnis understood. She'd felt totally useless for hours. She looked down at Michael, who gave her a hopeful smile. "Are the shops in the food court still open?"

"Not all of them, but the cookie place was when we came in."

"I'll walk out with you," Glynnis said.

They bought Michael his cookie and then slowly walked back to the management office. Gregg and Kat rejoined them a bit later. Gregg sat next to Glynnis and squeezed her hand. "Lieutenant O'Neill knows what he's doing, Glynnie. He'll find her."

But as the clock moved inexorably forward, Glynnis's hopes began to fade. If Livvy had been in the mall, surely they would have found her by now.

Finally Sabrina rose. "Glynnis, Gregg is going to stay with you, but I've got to go. I told Mrs. Phillips I'd be back for Samantha by ten-thirty, and it's almost that now."

Glynnis looked at her sister-in-law. "It's okay. I understand."

"How about if I take Michael with me? He can spend the night with us." Michael, head leaning against Glynnis's shoulder, had fallen asleep an hour ago. "In fact, *you* can spend the night with us, too. I don't think you should be alone if…" Sabrina, looking stricken, let her voice trail off.

"If they don't find Olivia tonight," Glynnis finished for her. Her eyes filled with tears. "I don't think they're going to."

"Oh, honey," Kat said. "They might. They haven't finished searching everywhere yet. That woman might have found a hiding place."

Glynnis shook her head. She knew Olivia was not in the mall, because if she had been, that woman—whoever she was—would not have been able to keep her quiet. Livvy was nothing if not vocal. If she was anywhere within hearing distance, the police would have discovered them.

Gregg, who'd been out front talking to the security people, walked back into the office. "You going to leave now?" he said to Sabrina.

"Yes. And if it's okay with Glynnis, I'll take Michael home with me."

"Yes, I think that's a good idea," Glynnis said. "But I won't be coming. When they finish here, I'm going home."

"You shouldn't be alone," Sabrina said. She looked at Kat. "Don't you agree?"

"Yes, I do."

"But what if Livvy or that woman who took her should call? I *have* to be there."

"How could they call? You said you didn't know the woman. Do you think she knows you?" This question came from Dan O'Neill, who had walked in behind Gregg.

"No, I don't think she knows me, although I can't be sure. But Olivia has an ID tag inside her jacket, sewed on to the lining in front. It's required at her day care center. The tag lists her name and our phone number."

"You're right, then. You should be at home," Kat said. "Don't worry, Sabrina. I'll stay with her. In fact, I'll call Bill right now and tell him." Out came her cell phone before Glynnis could even think of protesting. Not that she wanted to. She had no desire to be at home alone.

"I just came back to give you a status report," Lieutenant O'Neill said. "We've finished searching all the stores and the areas behind each store, as well as all the places in the inside of the mall. Everything is locked up now, and the mall's been emptied of all the shoppers and most of the store employees. The only ones left are a few maintenance people, the mall manager and his assistant, and the security personnel."

Glynnis's shoulders sagged. Even though she'd been afraid the woman who took Olivia was long gone, it was one thing to fear something and another thing entirely to know it for sure.

"Now that we're sure your daughter isn't in the mall," the lieutenant continued, "I called Chief Crandall, and he'll take care of issuing an Amber Alert. Do you know what that is?"

"It's a nationwide alert system, isn't it?" Gregg asked.

"Yes. A description of Olivia, along with her photo and the photo of the woman from the security tape will be faxed to primary radio stations under the Emergency Alert System. In turn, that information will be sent by them to area TV stations and radio stations. The radio stations will interrupt their programming to broadcast the information and TV and cable stations will run a 'crawl' on the screen along with the photos. In some places, the authorities will even incorporate electronic highway billboards. Every possible avenue will be covered. We're also setting up an 800-number hotline for people to call."

Glynnis nodded, unable to speak.

"Chief Crandall said to tell you we'll work on this night and day until we find your daughter."

"Th-thank you," Glynnis managed.

"Yes, thank you," Gregg and Sabrina echoed.

"Now I think you should go home and try to get some sleep," Dan O'Neill said.

But everyone in the room knew Glynnis wouldn't sleep tonight.

Not until Olivia was home again and safe in her own bed, would Glynnis be able to sleep again.

Chapter Three

"What if they don't find her?"

Gregg looked at his wife, who was in the process of undressing for bed. She'd voiced the question he'd tried not to think about, yet it had hovered at the back of his mind like a poisonous snake waiting to strike. "They'll find her."

"But Gregg," Sabrina insisted, her green eyes clouded with worry, "what if they *don't?*" She lowered her voice, although no one could possibly hear her. Samantha, their one-year-old, and Michael had been asleep for hours, and Glynnis was at her own home with Kat. "It would destroy Glynnis. I'm not sure she could survive." She shook her head. "God. Hasn't she been through *enough?* I know other people think she's really strong, and she *is,* but everyone has a breaking point." She unfastened her bra and tossed it on the bed.

"Let's not talk about this, okay?"

"I think we have to talk about it, because if the unthinkable happens and they don't find Livvy…or they find her—" Sabrina swallowed "—they…find her body…we have to be prepared. Glynnis will need us more than ever before." She reached for her nightgown.

Gregg knew Sabrina was right, but he didn't want to say the words out loud. To do so would give them a reality he couldn't acknowledge. "I'm sorry, I can't talk about this." He put the shoes he had just removed back on. "I know I won't sleep. I'm going for a walk. I need fresh air."

"Gregg, it's midnight."

"I won't be gone long."

"Gregg…"

"What?" He didn't look at her, although under normal circumstances he would rather look at Sabrina than anyone else in the world.

"Running away won't solve anything," she said gently.

"I'm not running away."

She didn't answer for a long moment. When she did, her voice was resigned. "All right, I'm sorry I pushed you. If you don't want to talk about it, I won't make you." She climbed into bed and reached for her reading glasses.

"Don't wait up," he said and then went out to the

entryway closet, where he donned his heavy jacket and gloves. After letting himself quietly out the back door, he headed down the driveway, all the while reassuring himself that he was right not to consider the worst.

The police would find Olivia. Dan O'Neill was a good cop. He was doing all the right things.

They *had* to find her. Nothing less was acceptable.

Sabrina was right about one thing, though. His sister had suffered enough. For a long time, Gregg had been furious with Ben March. If the older man hadn't already been dead, Gregg would have cheerfully strangled him with his bare hands for what he'd done to Glynnis.

But in the past year—mainly since Samantha was born—he'd gotten past his anger and started moving toward some semblance of understanding.

Gregg knew it couldn't have been easy for Ben to live with Sabrina's mother all those years. Even now, when she was supposedly happily married to her longtime love, she was a hard woman to be around.

It always amazed Gregg that Sabrina—who was one of the warmest women he'd ever known—could have been born to Isabel March, who, on her warmest day, was closer to the Arctic Circle than to the equator.

For Sabrina's sake, he was friendly to Isabel, but he'd never love her, although he was glad she and Sabrina had a decent relationship again.

But even though he understood Ben better now,

he still couldn't completely forgive him for what he'd put Glynnis through. Those days after he'd died, when Glynnis had found out she was not legally married to him and that he had another wife and an adult daughter, had been tough. But the worst days had come later, when all the well-wishers were gone and Glynnis had to face everyday life with two small children on her own. At least Ben had left the children well provided for.

As Sabrina had said, Glynnis was a strong woman. She'd proven that by everything she'd overcome: their parents' death, a disastrous relationship when she'd been in college, having to give up the baby that resulted from it, and then Ben's death and the truth about their marriage. A weaker woman might have broken. Glynnis hadn't. Throughout, no matter how much she was hurting, she'd gone on and made the best life she could.

This, though, could destroy her.

Gregg was so lost in his thoughts he didn't realize a car had pulled alongside him until he heard his name called. Turning, he recognized his cousin Steve's dark blue Ford Explorer.

"What're you doing out walking this late?" Steve said when Gregg came around to the driver's side to talk to him.

"I needed some air. You just coming home from the restaurant?" Steve had been Gregg's assistant for the past two and a half years and Gregg now wondered how he had ever managed without him.

"Yeah."

"We have a good night?"

"Real good. From seven-thirty on, all the tables stayed filled."

Gregg nodded. The first few years he'd owned Antonelli's, it had been touch and go as to whether he'd make it. The odds were against him; he'd always known that. Start-up restaurants didn't have a good track record. But with a combination of hard work and luck, he'd made Antonelli's into one of the most successful restaurants in the area.

"I take it there's no news," Steve said.

"No."

"Geez, Gregg, I'm sorry. Is there anything Maggie and I can do?" Maggie also worked for Gregg as first assistant to the chef. She and Steve had met at the restaurant, fallen in love and married a little over a year ago. Now she was pregnant with their first child.

Gregg didn't answer for a moment. He couldn't. He was all too aware of just how bad the situation was and how much worse it might get. "Pray," he finally said. "Pray hard."

"Yeah," Steve said softly. Then, "You want a ride back to the house?"

"Thanks, but I'm not ready to go back yet."

"Okay. You sure you're all right?"

"Yeah, I'm fine. You go on. Maggie'll be waiting."

Steve smiled. "All right. You comin' in tomorrow?"

"I don't know. We'll see."

"Well, don't worry about us. We can manage if

you want to stay with Glynnis. Everybody's torn up about this, you know."

"Yeah, I know." Glynnis had spent a lot of time at the restaurant since Ben had died, and the employees had pretty much adopted the kids. He smiled thinking how Jeff, their pastry chef, always let the kids roll out leftover dough and Trish, who was training to take Maggie's place as their sous-chef, taught Michaael to chop carrots.

Gregg watched as Steve drove off, then he headed toward the park. Since he didn't normally go to the restaurant before ten, in nice weather he always took Samantha to the park in the morning before he left for work. Many times, he'd included Olivia in their excursions, picking her up before Glynnis left for the school and then dropping her at her day care center on his way to the restaurant.

Samantha adored her older cousin. The two little girls always had a great time together, and Gregg enjoyed watching them. From the time of their birth, he'd been a surrogate father to Glynnis's children, and he knew they'd always occupy a special place in his heart.

Reaching the park, he walked down the main path to the pond and his favorite bench. As he'd known it would be, the park was deserted. It was too cold for lovers and too late for joggers. There weren't even any homeless people there, because last year, in co-operation with half a dozen businesses, the city had opened a shelter.

Locating the bench he'd come to think of as his, Gregg sat and pensively looked out over the pond. Moonlight shimmered across its dark, quiet surface. None of the lily pads or ducks that dotted the pond during the daytime were visible. He smiled, thinking how the girls loved those ducks. Whenever they came, they brought bread or crackers or popcorn to feed them. Samantha would squeal whenever one of them came too close, but Olivia wasn't afraid of them. She'd let them eat out of her hand if Gregg would allow it, but he was always afraid they might accidentally bite her, so he insisted that she put the food on the ground.

Soon the pond would freeze and the ducks would migrate somewhere warmer, but they always came back in the spring.

From somewhere across the pond, he heard the low, mournful who-who of an owl. The sound caused his chest to tighten.

Livvy. Where are you?

He felt so completely useless. If only he could do something to help. But what? What?

He thought about Samantha sleeping peacefully in her crib. Sabrina, probably lying awake in their bed worrying about him. Glynnis, frightened and sleepless in her house.

All of them needing him.

So what was he doing here?

He should be home with his wife and child. He should try to get some sleep so that he'd be better able to help Glynnis tomorrow.

Getting up, he began to run and didn't stop until he saw the welcoming lights of home.

Glynnis never did go to bed. Kat tried to make her, but she refused. She *did* change into an old pair of green velour sweatpants and a matching sweatshirt and put thick socks on her feet so she wouldn't be cold. But she spent the night curled up under an afghan on one of the love seats in the living room, and Kat spent the night on the other one.

As the night passed, Glynnis was aware of every sound. The ticking of the grandfather clock in the entryway. The hum of the refrigerator and the occasional clunk as the ice maker spit out its new supply of cubes. The distant drone of traffic on the interstate that cut through downtown. The wail of a siren somewhere in the distance. The rattle of the overhanging branches of the big maple tree in the side yard against the roof.

All so ordinary. The sounds of a normal night in a normal world. Only this wasn't a normal night or a normal world. Any world where some stranger could grab a child and walk off with her was a nightmare world.

Glynnis just prayed the nightmare would be over soon. That Olivia would be restored to her, safe and sound.

Where was she tonight? Was she warm? Safe? Was that woman taking care of her?

Glynnis's eyes filled with tears.

Please, God, watch over her. Watch over my baby.

"Glynnis?" Kat said softly. "You feel like talking?"

Glynnis surreptitiously wiped away the tears. "I thought you were sleeping."

"I tried, but too many thoughts are spinning around in my head."

"I know."

"If you want a sleeping pill, I've got some in my purse. They're just over the counter, nothing too strong."

"You carry sleeping pills around with you?"

"I grabbed them when I stopped at the house for my nightgown."

"No, I don't want one." How could she sleep when Olivia was out there somewhere, probably scared, probably crying for her?

"You want some hot chocolate or something? I could go make us some."

"No." *All I want is Olivia.* "But if you want some, go ahead."

"No. I just thought…" Her voice trailed off.

After that, Kat fell silent, and when another half hour went by, Glynnis thought she'd probably fallen asleep. Glynnis knew she should try to sleep, too, otherwise she'd be a zombie tomorrow, which would help no one.

But sleep wouldn't come.

At four-thirty Glynnis gave up. Quietly, so as not to wake Kat, she headed for the kitchen, where she put on a pot of coffee. She also took some frozen cinnamon rolls from the freezer so they'd be thawed by the time Kat awakened. Then she headed for her bathroom, where she splashed water on her face and brushed her teeth and hair. When she returned to the kitchen, the coffee was ready, its rich aroma filling the air.

Glynnis poured herself a cup, added powdered creamer and a packet of sweetener, then sat at the table. Slowly, she drank. She was just about finished when Kat, rubbing her eyes, padded into the kitchen.

"Did I wake you?" Glynnis said.

"The smell of coffee did." Kat walked over to the counter, yawned, got a mug out of the cupboard and poured herself a cup. She pulled a chair out and joined Glynnis at the table. "Did you get any sleep at all?"

Glynnis shrugged. "I dozed a little."

"You know, I was thinking. Maybe you should offer a reward for information."

For the first time since Olivia's disappearance, Glynnis felt a spark of excitement. "Kat, that's a *great* idea!"

"We could even take up a collection."

"That would take too long. Besides, it's not necessary. I can sell some of the stock Ben left the children. How much do you think I should offer? Would five thousand be enough? Or do you think I should offer ten thousand?"

"Ten thousand would probably get you more attention. But you know, we should probably ask Dan if this is a good idea. Maybe a reward will just muddy the waters."

"What do you mean?"

"You know, bring the nuts out of the woodwork with a lot of false leads."

"Oh, I hadn't thought about that. What time do you think it would be okay to call him?"

"What about right now?"

"Now? Kat, it's not even five o'clock. Won't he be sleeping?"

"Hon, Dan has probably been at work all night. I doubt he'd go home and sleep when Olivia is out there somewhere." So saying, Kat got up and went in search of her handbag. A few minutes later, she came back into the kitchen with her cell phone in hand. Quickly, she punched in some numbers.

"Hello? May I speak with Lieutenant O'Neill, please? Thank you." Grinning at Glynnis, she handed her the phone. "What'd I tell you? He's there. Here. You talk to him."

It warmed Glynnis to know he was there working in her behalf. A moment later, he came on the line.

"Lieutenant O'Neill."

"Dan? This is Glynnis. Glynnis March."

"Yeah. Hi, Glynnis. How you holding up?"

"I'm okay."

"Kat there with you?"

"Yes, sitting right across the table from me. Neither one of us could sleep."

"Yeah, I know the feeling."

"Um, Kat's the reason I'm calling. She had an idea, and we wanted to know what you thought about it."

"Oh?"

"Yes, we thought it might be helpful for me to offer a reward. You know, for information."

For a few seconds, he didn't answer, and Glynnis's heart sank. He didn't think it was a good idea.

Then he surprised her by saying, "You know, that's a pretty good idea. A reward might jog someone into remembering something they wouldn't ordinarily notice."

"You think so?"

"Yeah, I do. But to be enough incentive, the reward should be substantial, I'm afraid."

"I was thinking of ten thousand dollars."

He gave a low whistle. "That's substantial." Unspoken was a question. Could she afford that much money?

"Don't worry. I have the money. Thing is, how do we publicize this for maximum benefit?"

"Leave that to me. We'll call the TV and radio stations and the newspaper office. By tonight, everyone around here will have heard about it. And I wouldn't be surprised if the wire services pick it up."

"Okay." Glynnis actually smiled. Kat, who was watching and listening to the one-sided conversation, smiled back at her.

After hanging up, Glynnis said, "I think I'll go take a shower and get dressed."

"Good. I'll take mine when you're done."

As Glynnis headed for her bedroom, she felt ten times better than she'd felt just an hour earlier. She had a good feeling about this reward. And God willing, by tonight maybe Olivia would once again be sleeping in her own bed.

True to his word, Dan notified everyone he could think of about the reward Glynnis was offering. He spent the rest of the day questioning people and following what slim leads they were able to unearth. A couple of times he thought he was on to something, but nothing panned out. He was beginning to fear the woman who'd taken Olivia March had gotten away clean. No one had seen her leave the mall and so far, no one seemed to know who she was.

The bus station and cab companies were long shots, and Dan knew it. In all likelihood, the woman had come to the mall in her own car and left the same way. Without knowing what kind of car she drove, there was no way to trace her. Trouble was, the mall had been really busy the day before. A woman and child—even if the child were crying—would not stand out. Hell, Dan had seen half a dozen crying kids when he'd arrived at the mall yesterday. Crying kids were the norm, not the exception.

No one else had any luck, either. All in all, it was a damned frustrating day. Their only hope was the reward Glynnis was offering. News of it would reach the majority of people tonight, on the evening news.

At five o'clock, Chief Crandall walked out to Dan's desk. "Go home, Dan. You've been at it for what, twenty-four, twenty-five straight hours? You need to get some sleep."

"Not sure I *can* sleep, Chief."

"Well, try. You're no good to me if you're punchy, and without sleep, you're gonna be. Don't worry. I'll call you if anything happens."

Dan didn't want to go, but he could see by the expression on the chief's face that he wasn't going to take no for an answer, so reluctantly Dan stood and put on his coat. "You've got my cell phone number? In case I'm not home?"

"Dan…"

"I just thought I might stop by the mother's house on my way home, that's all."

"Fine. But make sure you get some sleep after that, you hear? And yes, I've got your cell phone number."

Dan knew Glynnis's neighborhood. One of his best friends from high school had lived one street away from where she lived now. It was the kind of neighborhood working class families aspired to, near Whitney Park and the public golf course. It wasn't far from downtown, so it only took him a few minutes to get there, locate her home and park in front. She lived in an attractive red-brick-and-frame, one-story bungalow. A giant blue spruce tree stood on one side of the house. A black Honda Passport sat in the driveway. Dan had wondered if his sister was still there, but he didn't see her red Accord anywhere.

Dan took note of the Christmas welcome mat on the front stoop. It was going to be one helluva lousy holiday for Glynnis and her family if they didn't find her little girl. On that somber thought, he walked to the door and rang the doorbell.

Only a few seconds went by before the door opened. He wanted to kick himself when he saw the expectant light in her eyes. He should have called first.

"I'm sorry," he said. "There's nothing new. I just stopped by to see how you're doing."

"Oh." The light died. She shrugged. "I'm okay."

She didn't look okay. She looked like hell. Tired, pale and worried. Despite this, she looked younger than she had the day before, probably because today she wore no makeup and was dressed in jeans and a sweater, with her hair tied back in a ponytail. The sweater, in some kind of reddish-brown shade, complemented her eyes and hair.

"I also thought I'd give you an update of what we've done so far."

"Come on in, then."

He followed her into the house, his eye—trained to notice even minute details—taking in the warm colors and hominess of the interior, from the beautiful wood floors to the comfortable-looking furniture to the family photos on the walls.

He stopped in front of an eleven-by-fourteen framed photo of a chunky infant with a dimpled smile. "This is Livvy."

Her eyes widened. "How can you tell? She's only eleven months old in that picture."

"The dimples gave it away."

She made a brave attempt at a smile. "I love her dimples," she said softly. "They reflect her mischievous personality."

Next to that photograph was another, this time of her son, who looked to be about three. He, too, was grinning, but even with the wide smile on his face, it was easy to see this child was much more serious than his younger sister.

As if she'd read his mind, she said, "Michael bears the weight of the world on his shoulders."

Dan looked at her. "Like his mother?"

She blinked. "How did you know that?"

"I'm pretty good at reading people." Once he hadn't been.

She nodded. "I guess you have to be in your line of work."

"It helps."

For a moment, she didn't say anything. Then, so softly, he had to strain to hear her, she whispered, "I'm so scared."

"I know you are. That's one of the reasons I came by. I wanted to assure you that every law enforcement officer in the county, maybe even in the state, is out there looking for your daughter. It may take awhile, but we'll find her."

She nodded.

Just then the grandfather clock standing in the

corner of the foyer began to chime. Dan realized the local news would be starting now. "You have a TV set, don't you?"

"Yes."

"Want to watch the news? See what they say about the reward?"

"Oh, yes, of course."

He followed her into the living room and sat on one of the green print love seats, while she picked up a remote from the coffee table and aimed it at the television set. A moment later, the local NBC newsroom flared into life. Bill Mendoza, the male anchor, was giving an update on the national budget crisis and the headway made that day by a resolution being debated in the House of Representatives. When he finished, Sherry Hudson, the pretty blond coanchor, held up the photo of Olivia that Glynnis had given him yesterday. Talking rapidly but succinctly, she recapped yesterday's events, then said, "Olivia's family is offering a reward of ten thousand dollars to anyone with information leading to the girl's recovery."

She went on to explain who they should call and how they could claim the reward. When she finished, the 800 number flashed on the screen, superimposed over the photo of Olivia.

"I have a four-year-old daughter of my own," Sherry Hudson said, "and Bill has twin two-year-old daughters, don't you, Bill?"

He nodded solemnly.

"I know how I'd feel if my daughter was missing. Please, all you viewers out there, if you can think of anything, *anything,* that will help return Olivia to her family, call the 800 number or the Ivy Police Department. Let's bring Olivia home and give her family a wonderful Christmas."

When the anchor finished and moved on to other news, Dan saw that Glynnis was crying.

Impulsively, he got up and walked over to where she sat. Reaching down, he took her hand and pulled her to her feet. Then he did something he knew he shouldn't. He put his arms around her and held her while she cried. At first, she was stiff, but gradually she relaxed against him and allowed him to comfort her.

Holding her trembling body, Dan silently repeated his pledge. He would find this woman's daughter and he would bring her safely home. He had to.

Chapter Four

Dan hadn't slept in forty-eight hours. He was running on caffeine, Advil and little else. And a couple of times during the past five days, he'd almost bought a pack of cigarettes but somehow he'd managed to resist the impulse.

Good thing, he thought now, or he'd have a much worse headache than he had. Not to mention the fact it had taken him weeks of misery to finally kick the habit—something he had no wish to repeat.

Taking a large swallow of his rapidly cooling coffee, he swiveled his chair around and stared out the window. On the best days, there wasn't much of a view—just the parking lot for the station—and today even that was obscured by the snow, which had been falling for hours before stopping about an hour ago.

Although it was the first snow of the season, something Dan normally enjoyed, he took no pleasure from today's accumulation. The only thing he could think about right now was Olivia March.

He knew the odds against finding her safe were steadily increasing. Statistics showed that if a child wasn't found within the first twenty-four hours, the chances of finding that child alive grew increasingly slimmer over time. However, the fact she'd been taken by a woman was in their favor, because abductions by women were usually not sexually related, and the chances of finding Olivia alive and unharmed were much greater than if she'd been abducted by a man.

But that would be small comfort to Glynnis and the rest of Olivia's family. Dan couldn't imagine what Christmas would be like if that child was still missing.

What else can I do to find her?

That was the question he'd asked himself over and over again. They all had. Every single cop in the department wanted to find Olivia March, and they'd all been working hard to accomplish it.

What else? What haven't we done? What stone haven't we overturned? What lead might we have missed?

He ticked off a mental checklist. They'd searched the mall thoroughly. Questioned everyone there who might have seen the woman and child. Interviewed the ticket agent at the bus station and looked through all the records of who had bought tickets.

Olivia March's picture had been plastered everywhere: on telephone poles, in shop windows, in the local newspaper and the newspapers of neighboring towns, on TV shows and anywhere else they could think of. An Amber Alert had gone out, with descriptions of both the abductor and the child. And they'd publicized the reward money everywhere.

They'd followed every lead they'd gotten. Several of the leads had been promising, but in the end, they'd led to nothing.

Dan didn't know what else to do. In the beginning, he'd hoped for a swift conclusion. Now all he hoped for was a positive resolution, no matter how much time it took.

He thought about the way Glynnis had looked yesterday, the last time he'd seen her. Her face had been haggard, her eyes bleak. She looked as if she hadn't slept at all, and he doubted she was eating much.

He knew she hadn't gone to work today, because he'd talked to her this morning, and she was still at home. Of course he understood how impossible it was for her to teach classes when she was worried sick—not knowing if her daughter was alive or dead.

Dead.

That was the thought that haunted Dan, that Olivia March might not be alive. That when they did find her, they'd find a body.

Dan never prayed. He'd lost his faith a long time ago. But right now, something very like prayer tumbled through his mind.

Please let us find her alive. Please let us bring her back to her mother.

No one should have to endure the death of a child. Even before his own beloved child died, he'd known it was the worst thing that could ever happen to a person. A child dying went against the laws of nature. Children were supposed to bury parents, not vice versa.

"Dan! Line Three. It's someone about the March girl," Elena's excited voice called. An eternal optimist, she was always certain that the most recent tip would be the one that finally panned out.

Dan punched the blinking line. "Lieutenant O'Neill."

"Um, hello? Are you the policeman in charge of that missing little girl case?"

"Yes, ma'am. Have you got some information?"

"Well, I'm not sure. See, what happened is—"

"First, what's your name, ma'am?" he interrupted.

"Oh, sorry. My name is Chapman. Virginia Chapman. And I live in Carrey." Carrey was a neighboring town, eight miles west of Ivy. She went on to give him her address and phone number. "I own a little neighborhood grocery store out on the far north side. Chapman's Market. And, um, there's this girl, she's been comin' in for a while now. Her name is Tammy. Not sure about her last name 'cause she always pays cash. But she lives in a trailer park—well, I guess they call it a mobile home park—not far from my store. I do know that, 'cause we talked about it once, and she said when her husband got out of the Army, she hoped they could buy a house, 'cause they had this little girl and she didn't want her growin' up in no trailer park. She wanted her to have a better life than she'd had." The Chapman woman paused as if she expected him to say something.

"And? Do you think this girl knows something about Olivia March's disappearance?" Dan prompted.

"Well, the thing is, in all the times I've seen her, I haven't seen no little girl with her. Which I thought was odd, but the one time I asked about her, Tammy got this funny look. I don't know what the word is to describe it. Shifty, maybe? No, that's not right. More like confused. And all she said was that the baby was sick and she couldn't take her out. I wondered who was watching the kid, but I didn't feel like I could ask. I mean, I didn't know Tammy. She was just a customer and not from around Carrey, either, I don't think. We get a lot of these Army people in Carrey, you know, with the base bein' so close and all."

Dan was becoming excited, and he wanted to hurry the woman along. Yet he knew that you couldn't hurry some civilians because if you did, you might lose an important bit of information, so he only said, "And what makes you think this woman might have something to do with the missing March girl?"

"Well, several things. I mean, that picture of her

on the TV was really fuzzy and all, but I could see that the woman who took that girl had kind of spiked-up hair, and that's the way Tammy wears her hair. Plus, she's young and skinny like that woman. But the biggest thing is, yesterday she came into the store and she had a little girl with her. Now I wouldn't have thought a thing of it, but that little one looked like that picture they've been showing on the TV, plus when I smiled at her and said well, this must be Tiffany—that's what Tammy told me her little girl's name was one time—the little girl frowned kind of funny. Then she said something quietlike and it sounded to me like Libby. And I know I read that the missing girl's mother calls her Livvy."

Now Dan's adrenaline was really pumping. This was the most promising lead they'd gotten so far.

"Anyway, I just thought I should call you. Maybe you could check it out. 'Course, I'd hate if I was falsely accusing Tammy, but still…I can't imagine what it'd be like if your little girl was taken. I know how I woulda felt if something like that had happened to my Cheryl. Why, I'd've been crazy wild. That little girl's mother must be scared to death about now."

"How did the child seem?"

"Well, she seemed fine. She wasn't cryin' or nothin'. Tammy was holding her in her arms, and the little girl had her own arms around Tammy's neck." Now Virginia Chapman spoke hesitantly, as if unsure of herself.

"Do you know the name of the mobile home park?"

"Yes. It's called Sycamore Mobile Home Village, on Sycamore Road out near that abandoned airfield. You know the one?"

"No, but I'm sure there are people here who do. How big is that mobile home park, do you know?"

"There's maybe twenty-five, thirty mobile homes there. There's a manager on site. Her name is Brenda Nuttley."

"Thank you, Ms. Chapman. You've been a big help. We'll go and check this out."

"You'll let me know what happens?"

"Yes, we will. And if it turns out that the little girl you saw really is Olivia March, you'll be eligible to collect the reward posted by the family."

"That's not why I called."

"I know that. But you'll still be eligible."

"Well, okay. Now you won't hurt Tammy, will you?"

"All we want to do is question her." Dan hoped she wouldn't realize he had evaded a direct answer, but he couldn't in good conscience say they wouldn't hurt the woman. Especially when he had no idea what they might encounter.

After hanging up, he went in to talk to Chief Crandall, who knew exactly where the airfield was that Virginia Chapman had mentioned. "Take three men with you," the chief said. "I'll call Sheriff Russo and let him know what's going down."

Carrey was too small a town to have a separate police department, so the county sheriff was the chief law enforcement officer for the area.

"I'll have him and a few of his men meet you out there." The chief reached for the phone. "What do you think, Dan? Did this woman sound credible?"

"Yeah, she did. But I *am* bothered by one thing she said. The little girl was hugging this Tammy woman. That bothered the Chapman woman, too."

"Well, you know…" The chief rubbed his chin. "I got a three-year-old grandson and he takes to other people pretty fast, especially if they're nice to him. So if this Tammy person has been kind to the March kid, it's not such a stretch to think she'd take to her."

Dan nodded. "Yeah, you're probably right." He hoped the chief was right. He'd sure as hell hate to go scaring some woman if the kid really did belong to her.

It took Dan and his men close to thirty minutes to get to Carrey and find the mobile home park. When they arrived, two cruisers marked with the county sheriff's emblem were waiting near the entrance.

Dan parked and then he, Romeo and the two patrolmen accompanying them got out and tromped through the snow to where the sheriff stood.

They introduced themselves and Sheriff Russo, a big, swarthy man who looked like he could have been a weight lifter, said, "I've already talked to Brenda, the manager. She says the Wilkerson woman lives in number fourteen, near the back."

"Wilkerson? That's her last name?"

"Yep. There's no other Tammys here. Brenda knew who I meant right away. She said she saw the child yesterday and wondered about her, but figured it was a niece or the child of a friend or something."

Dan nodded.

"We waited till you got here," Russo said. "Figured this was your collar. You'd want to be the one to find her if it really is the missing kid."

"Thanks."

The sheriff beckoned to the two deputies who were in the other car and the seven men, led by Dan, walked into the mobile home park. There were four rows of homes, and number fourteen was the last one in the second row. It was a neat unit, with green curtains covering the windows and a little covered patio area to the right of the front door. Several lawn chairs were folded up and leaning against the side of the mobile home.

All the officers except Dan had their weapons drawn and ready. Dan knew he was taking a chance, but he didn't want to frighten the woman, so he left his gun in its holster, trusting that his backup would protect him.

He climbed the two steps leading to the front door and rapped three times. He could hear music playing inside, but whether it was from a radio or a TV set, he couldn't tell. He rapped again.

A moment later, a young woman opened the door an inch or so. "Yes?" she said in a high, girlish voice.

"Mrs. Wilkerson? Tammy Wilkerson?"

"Yes." She didn't seem frightened or alarmed.

Dan held up his badge. "I'm Lieutenant Dan O'Neill from the Ivy Police Department. I'd like to ask you a few questions."

She frowned, opening the door wider. "Why? Has something happened?"

Still no alarm in her eyes, which Dan could see were a light blue. She certainly fit the profile of the woman on the tape. In her teens or early twenties, thin, and definitely wearing a spiked hairdo. She was dressed in faded jeans, a dark blue sweatshirt and dark blue socks. There were no shoes on her feet. She was the most nonthreatening-looking possible perp Dan had ever seen, with the most innocent-looking eyes.

"Nothing for you to be alarmed about. We just need to check something out. I understand you have a little girl?"

Now Tammy Wilkerson smiled. "Yes. Tiffany. She's three."

Dan nodded. "I'd like to see her, if you don't mind."

The smile faded. "But why? She's sleeping, and I don't like to disturb her."

"I'm sorry, but I really need to see her."

"But she hasn't been feeling good, and I don't want to wake her up."

"This won't take long." Something about this woman wasn't right. Dan almost always knew when a suspect was lying, but nothing about this girl seemed false. Either she was a very good actress or she really believed the girl was hers.

"Well, okay," she said, but she was shaking her head, concern clouding her expression. For the first time, she seemed to notice the other officers. "Do...do you want to come in? It's too cold to bring her outside."

Dan looked at Sheriff Russo, indicating he should come, too. "Thank you." Dan followed her inside. Russo came immediately after him.

The interior of the mobile home was very clean and neat, just like the outside. A child's pink sip cup sat next to a bowl of animal crackers on the little table in the kitchen area.

Tammy Wilkerson led them through the main part of the mobile home to the bedroom area in the back where a child, covered by a blanket and hugging a teddy bear, lay curled up on a double bed.

Tammy smiled. "Here she is," she whispered. Lovingly, she touched the tangled curls on the little girl's head.

"I'm really sorry, Mrs. Wilkerson," Dan said. "But you'll have to wake her up, because I need to ask her some questions."

She shook her head, forming the word no silently.

He couldn't help feeling sorry for her. She seemed so completely unaware of why they were there.

"Sorry, little lady," Russo said behind him. "But we need to talk to the child."

With a resigned look, she reached over and gently shook the child's shoulders, saying softly, "Tiffany, sweetheart, you have to wake up now. Wake up, Tiffany."

Slowly the child's eyes opened. Unfocused for a moment, they gradually cleared. Hazel. They were hazel.

Dan's heart knocked in his chest. If that wasn't Olivia March lying there, then it was her twin. She looked exactly like the pictures he'd seen in Glynnis's home.

The little girl stretched and finally saw Dan and Sheriff Russo. Her eyes got big and she shrank back against the bed.

"Hi," Dan said softly. "Don't be afraid. I'm a policeman. See?" He held up his badge. "I just wanted to say hello and ask you a couple of questions, okay?"

The child's eyes darted to Tammy. Tammy smiled down at her. "It's okay, sweetheart. You can talk to the policeman. He won't hurt you."

If this wasn't the most bizarre thing Dan had ever seen, he didn't know what was. This woman didn't have a clue about what was going on. Dan would swear she really believed this kid was hers. For just a second, he felt uncertain. As if he was the one wrong here. Maybe this little girl *was* Tiffany Wilkerson, like her supposed mother had said. They say that everyone has a double somewhere. Maybe this child just looked like Olivia March.

Could that be?

"What's your name, honey?" he said. When she didn't answer, he asked again, more firmly this time.

The child jammed her thumb in her mouth and spoke around it. What she said sounded like "Wivvy." But it could have been a garbled version of Tiffany. "Livvy?" he asked. "Is that what your name is? Olivia?"

"No! Her name is *Tiffany*," Tammy Wilkerson said. "I told you."

Dan reached down and gently pulled the thumb out of the child's mouth. "Olivia?" he said again. "Are you Olivia? Do you have an older brother named Michael?"

"Michael!" A huge smile split her face, complete with dimples. She sat up and looked around. "Michael?" The smile disappeared, and her face puckered up.

"Come here, honey," Dan said, reaching for her. "I'll take you to Michael."

"No!" Tammy Wilkerson clutched at his arm. "No. You can't take her. She's my baby. What are you *doing?* Where are you going?"

"Ma'am," Sheriff Russo said. "You're going to have to come with us."

"No! Stop it! Tiffany!" Tears rolled down Tammy Wilkerson's face as she reached toward Olivia.

Olivia hid her face against Dan's neck.

"Mrs. Wilkerson," Dan said, "this little girl isn't your daughter. Her name is Olivia March, and you took her from the Ivy Mall. Her mother is scared to death."

"That's not true! It's not!" She lunged for Dan and tried to wrest Olivia from his arms.

Sheriff Russo grabbed her, putting his arms around her and pinning hers to her sides. "Go on, take the kid outside," he said. "Now you just calm down, Miz Wilkerson."

"Let me go!" she cried.

"Tell you what. I'll let you go if you stop struggling. Then you can go get your daughter's birth certificate and any other documentation or pictures you might have, and we'll all go to my office and look 'em over, and if that little girl really *is* yours, we'll find out."

"This blanket isn't enough to keep her warm," Dan pointed out. "She had a coat." Gentling his voice, he said, "Where's her coat, Mrs. Wilkerson?"

"This isn't right," she cried. "You can't just come into a person's house and take her child. It's not right!"

While she was talking, her eyes had darted to the other wall, where Dan saw louvered doors. Walking over, he opened the closet and immediately spied the bright yellow down jacket Glynnis had described. Without letting go of Olivia, he removed the jacket and looked inside. Sure enough, there was the label with Olivia's name and address. Holding the coat up so the sheriff could see it, Dan showed him the label.

Russo nodded grimly. "You go on. Take the girl

home. I'll go along with your patrolmen. We'll take Ms. Wilkerson into the station for you."

Dan didn't wait any longer. He couldn't wait to take Olivia home and to see the look on Glynnis's face when he walked in the door.

Glynnis knelt by the boxes of Christmas ornaments stacked in the hallway. Tears filled her eyes. She'd gotten the ornaments down from the attic on Saturday. The kids had been so excited. They'd planned to buy a tree on Sunday afternoon and decorate it Sunday night.

In the blink of an eye, everything had changed.

Today was Thursday.

Five days since Livvy had been taken. Each moment of each day had been agonizing, exhausting, terrifying.

Where was she?

Reaching into the box, Glynnis lifted out a glittery silver star. The stars were Livvy's favorite ornaments. Last year she'd insisted on hanging them herself, even though Glynnis had had to lift her and cup her hand so that she could get the ornaments to stay on the branches. Even at two years old, she'd been stubbornly independent.

Please God...

I can't lose her. Please let her be okay....

"Glynnis?"

Glynnis turned to look at Kat, who had practically been living there the past five days. When Glynnis had told her it wasn't necessary for her to stay, Kat said she'd cancelled all her appointments and wasn't going anywhere until Olivia was back home. A real estate agent, she had the luxury of not working if she didn't want to. Of course, as she had pointed out once, when she didn't work, she didn't make any money.

Now she said, "I fixed some tuna salad."

"Thanks, but I'm not hungry."

"Hon, you have to keep up your strength. If you don't eat, you're going to get sick."

"I don't care."

Kat pursed her mouth. Glynnis knew she was counting to ten, telling herself to be patient. "Now look," she finally said, "you're being unreasonable. Not to mention the fact that you'll be in no shape to take care of your children when they're back home." Michael was still at Gregg and Sabrina's. Glynnis had agreed with them that he was better off staying there for the duration.

Glynnis swiped at her eyes. "Kat…"

Kat walked over and put her arm around Glynnis's shoulder. "What, hon?"

"What if…what if she doesn't come home?"

"She's coming home," Kat said fiercely. "Don't even *think* of anything else."

"But it's been so long…"

"Dan will find her. I know he will."

"But what if he *doesn't?*"

"He *will*. I know—" She broke off as the doorbell rang.

Both women turned.

Through the glass side panel, Glynnis saw Dan's face peering through. For a moment, she wanted to shout at him, tell him to go away and not come back until he brought Olivia home.

But just as quickly as her anger flared, it faded away. Dan was doing his best. Besides, it wasn't his fault Olivia was missing. It was hers.

Wearily, she opened the door.

"Oh, my God!" Kat said, covering her mouth with her hand.

Glynnis stared in stunned amazement.

"Mommy!"

Glynnis knew she would never, not if she lived a million years, forget the sheer joy of that moment. Olivia's happy face. Dan's huge smile. Kat's exclamations behind her. And her own heart, pounding away in thankfulness.

Tears running down her face, she reached for Olivia. "Oh, Livvy, Livvy, you're okay. You're okay."

"Mommy, you crying." Livvy patted Glynnis's face.

"I'm crying because I'm so happy." Glynnis buried her face in Livvy's soft neck, breathing in the familiar smells. When she had herself under some semblance of control, she raised her face and met Dan's gaze. He was still standing outside. "Oh, Dan, I'm sorry. I'm so happy, I'm not thinking straight. Come in. Come in and tell me everything. How did you find her? Where was she?"

For the next hour, as Dan talked and filled them

in on everything, Glynnis held Olivia tightly on her lap. She must have kissed her a hundred times. Finally Livvy squirmed away, saying, "Mommy, I thirsty."

Kat jumped up. "What do you want to drink, darling? Juice? Milk?"

"Juice," Olivia said.

"Milk," Glynnis said. Then she laughed and hugged Olivia harder. "Oh, give her juice. I don't care. Give her anything she wants."

Olivia struggled to get down. Reluctantly, Glynnis released her. The sound of her running feet as she followed Kat out of the room was the sweetest sound Glynnis had ever heard.

When they were gone, Glynnis turned to Dan. "Dan, I'll never be able to thank you enough."

He smiled. "No thanks necessary. I just did my job. What any good cop would do."

"Maybe, but I'll never forget it. Never. I wish there was some way I could repay you."

"Just seeing the look on your face when you saw Olivia was payment enough," he replied softly.

"She looks good, don't you think?"

"Yes, I do. The Wilkerson woman took good care of her. I don't think she lacked for anything."

Glynnis nodded. She kept thinking about Tammy Wilkerson. How awful to lose your baby as she had. Glynnis remembered how devastated she'd been all those years ago, but at least she'd known *her* little one was going to a good family. Still, you never forgot. Your arms never stopped aching for the child that wasn't there.

But today wasn't a day for sad memories. Today was a day for making happy memories.

Just then, Kat and Livvy returned and Dan stood. "I need to get back to the station. Sheriff Russo was taking the Wilkerson woman there."

Glynnis walked him to the door. "I feel so sorry for the girl if she really thought Livvy was her daughter."

"I do, too," he said. "She certainly seemed to."

"You'll let me know what happens with her?"

"Of course. I'll call you later."

"Thank you."

He smiled down at her. "Now you'd better get back to your daughter."

"Yes. But before I do I just wanted to tell you again that I'll never forget what you've done for us. Never." Once again, her emotions threatened to overwhelm her. Without conscious thought, she slid her arms around his waist, laid her face against his chest and hugged him. After only a second's hesitation, his arms closed around her and he returned the embrace, holding her close for a long moment. Glynnis closed her eyes and allowed herself to revel in the warmth and feeling of safety that being held by Dan produced. When they slowly drew apart, she couldn't help experiencing a sense of loss.

Murmuring goodbye, he walked out.

Standing in the doorway, she watched until his car disappeared from view. Only then did she close the door and return to the living room and her daughter.

Chapter Five

Glynnis could hardly stand to let Olivia out of her sight. When bedtime came, Glynnis asked the children if they wanted to have a picnic and camp out in her room that night.

"Yay!" Olivia clapped her hands, giving Glynnis one of her irresistible grins.

Michael pretended he was too old for anything as babyish as sleeping in his mother's room, but finally he gave in to the excitement of the preparations. Glynnis made hot chocolate with marshmallows and popped popcorn, then spread an old quilt on the floor, and the three of them sat on it to eat and watch Olivia's favorite video—Walt Disney's *The Jungle Book*.

After an intermission to clean up the food, slip

into pajamas, brush teeth and say prayers, they piled into Glynnis's bed and snuggled under the quilts to watch the remainder of the video. Olivia was so tired, she fell asleep before her favorite part, where Baloo teaches Mowgli the *Bare Necessities*. Michael managed to stay awake until the end, but just barely.

Although she was completely worn out from days of trauma and very little rest, sleep didn't come easily to Glynnis. She kept looking at her darling children and thinking how much she loved them and how frighteningly close she'd come to losing one of them. She kept touching their faces: serious, sweet-natured Michael, her little man who worried about everyone and everything, and independent, stubborn, thoroughly charming Olivia, who would probably give Glynnis many gray hairs before she grew up.

She considered it a privilege to be their mother, to have the opportunity to teach them and mold them and, she hoped, see them grow into productive, intelligent, caring adults. Once she'd had to forfeit that privilege, so she knew just how precious it was.

Oh, Ben, I wish you could see them now. You'd be so proud of them. They're such wonderful children.

Thank God they were both safe. God and Dan O'Neill. She smiled, thinking about the detective. The image of him, standing on her doorstep, holding Olivia, would be forever branded upon Glynnis's mind.

She knew the entire police department had worked hard, but he'd been the driving force behind the search for Olivia. He'd been the one who wouldn't let any lead go by without checking it out. And he'd been the one to find her. How could she ever properly thank the man who had given her back her life?

She was still thinking about Dan when she finally fell asleep a little after midnight.

Though there was only one day left before Christmas vacation officially began, the next morning Glynnis couldn't bear the thought of sending the children to school, not after all the three of them had been through. Today, she decided, they deserved a carefree day of fun. They could shop for their Christmas tree and decorate it. Maybe, if there was time, she'd even put up some lights outside. It wasn't too late. There were still nine days until Christmas.

While the children were still sleeping, Glynnis poured herself a cup of coffee and drank it while she read the morning paper.

The front page headline announced Olivia's safe return, and next to her picture, there was a long story detailing the events from her abduction to her recovery. Though Glynnis already knew the story had a happy ending, her heartbeat quickened at the sight, and she thought once again how horribly different the headline and story might have read. She'd barely finished reading the story when the phone rang.

"How are you this morning?" Gregg said in greeting.

She smiled. "Wonderful."

"Did you sleep well?"

"I had a hard time falling asleep. Too keyed up, I guess. But I slept soundly once I did."

"Good. You know, I've been thinking. We need to celebrate. How about a party at the restaurant tomorrow night, maybe at six so people can bring their kids?"

"Oh, Gregg, that's a great idea."

"You decide who you want to be there, then call me and give me your list, okay?"

"All right."

"Before we hang up, Sabrina wants to talk to you."

When Sabrina came on the line, she said, "Are you going in to work today?"

"No. After what we've been through, I could use a day to regroup with the kids. I'm going to call Dean Clemmons in a minute and make sure it's okay, but I don't think he'll care. I think we'll go buy our Christmas tree and put it up."

"Want some help?"

"Sure. That would be great."

They made arrangements for Sabrina to come by about ten. After hanging up, Glynnis looked at the clock. Seeing it was after eight, she decided to call her boss, who was always at his desk early. As anticipated, he gave her no problem over taking the day off.

Before saying goodbye, Glynnis invited the dean and his wife to come to the celebration party at Antonelli's, and he said he'd be there.

After that, she poured herself a second cup of coffee, then began making up her list for the party. Halfway through, she heard the children giggling, and a few moments later, Michael, followed by Livvy, came racing into the kitchen.

"Hey, slow down. Where's the fire?" She gave them both hugs and kisses. There was nothing sweeter, she thought as she buried her face in Olivia's neck and nuzzled, than a child still redolent from sleep. "Guess what? I'm making waffles."

"Waffles?" Michael's eyes lit up.

Livvy grinned. "Waffess." *L* was another letter she had trouble pronouncing.

"Bacon, too?" Michael asked.

"Oh, honey, I'm sorry. I haven't been to the supermarket in a week, and we don't have any bacon."

He frowned, then shrugged.

She bit back a smile. That was Michael. He might be disappointed, but he was so practical; he knew pouting didn't change anything.

Glynnis plugged in the waffle iron and while it was heating, she got the children settled at the table. "What kind of juice do you want this morning?"

Michael considered. "Orange juice," he finally said.

"What about you, Livvy?"

"Apple spider!"

Glynnis chuckled. Ever since they'd had apple cider in September, Olivia had used her own version of the name, even though Glynnis had explained numerous times that apple juice was not the same as apple cider. Glancing at Michael, she saw he had rolled his eyes.

Once the children were busy eating their breakfast, Glynnis returned to her list. Suddenly she grinned. She'd thought of the perfect way to show Dan O'Neill how grateful she was. He would be the guest of honor at the party!

She waited until nine before calling him, debating whether to try him directly on his cell phone or to call the station. Deciding he wouldn't appreciate being disturbed if he was home sleeping, she called the station.

"Lieutenant O'Neill."

"Oh, you're there. I expected to get the operator. This is Glynnis March."

"I recognized your voice. Good morning. How are you today?"

"Great, thanks to you."

"How's Olivia doing?"

"Well, right now she's got a huge amount of waffle stuffed into her mouth and syrup running down her chin."

Dan laughed. "Sounds like she's doing just fine."

"I don't think she's any the worse for wear after her experience."

"Good."

"What about the woman who took her?"

"We located her husband. He's stationed in the Middle East, but after what happened, he thinks he'll be able to come home. Apparently after their daughter died over a year ago, she was in bad shape. But then she seemed to improve, and he thought she was okay. Obviously, she's not."

"What's going to happen to her?"

"I don't know. She spent the night at the county hospital under police guard, and today the staff psychiatrist will talk to her. Guess they'll decide after that whether to file charges against her or to recommend medical treatment."

"I hope she gets treatment. I don't want her to go to jail."

"Even after what she put you through?"

"It's over now. And like you said, she's obviously ill. As long as something is done so she doesn't hurt any other family, I'll be happy."

"Some mothers might not be so charitable."

"What point is there in wanting revenge? If the woman's sick, she's sick. Besides, I have my daughter back and she's in great shape. That's all I really care about."

Just then said daughter knocked over her sip cup of milk, and the top, which must not have been put on securely, popped off and milk splattered everywhere.

"Oh, no!" Glynnis said. "Listen, Dan, I've gotta go. Livvy just spilled her milk. But I wanted to tell you. We're having a celebration party tomorrow night at Antonelli's, and you're invited. It starts at six o'clock." With one hand, she grabbed some paper towels from the roll and began mopping up the mess. Olivia, totally unconcerned, continued eating her waffle. "Can you make it?"

"Sure. I'd love to come."

"Do you know where Antonelli's is?"

"Yes, I've eaten there before."

"Great. So we'll see you tomorrow?"

"I wouldn't miss it."

Glynnis was smiling when she disconnected the call. As she finished cleaning up Olivia's mess, she debated calling Chief Crandall and inviting him, along with some of the other officers involved in the search, but she decided not to. She would send a formal thank-you note and some cookies and brownies from the bakery to the station.

But for the party, she only wanted Dan.

Since Dan had been back in Ivy, he'd eaten at Antonelli's several times. He'd been pleasantly surprised, finding the restaurant compared favorably to his favorite Italian eateries in Chicago.

He was looking forward to the evening. Not just because he was happy about the outcome of the Olivia March case, but because he was curious to see Glynnis in a normal setting. So far, he'd only seen her in a highly emotional state, certainly not at her best.

So it was with a heightened sense of anticipation that he entered her brother's restaurant.

"Dan O'Neill," he said to the pretty, dark-haired hostess. "I'm here for the Antonelli party."

"You're the one who found Olivia!"

"Not just me. Everyone in the department worked to bring her back."

"Oh, c'mon," she said coyly, flirting a bit. "Don't be so modest. Gregg told me all about you."

It made Dan uncomfortable to be singled out when all he'd done was the job he was paid to do. Like most of the cops he knew, he considered himself part of a team. Maybe to civilians it seemed outdated and corny, but there really was a brotherhood, especially when it came to outcomes that were successful. He shrugged awkwardly.

"They're all over there…" She motioned to a dining area closed off from the main dining room by french doors. "Follow me." She gave him another flirty smile. "I understand you're pretty new to Ivy."

"Yes, I've only been here a few months."

"Well, we're so glad to have you. Good-looking single men are always welcome. You *are* single, aren't you?"

He grinned, relaxed now that she had stopped focusing on Olivia's case. "Yes, I'm single."

"And I'm Janine."

Now he laughed. "Nice to meet you, Janine."

"Oh, it's *my* pleasure."

She opened one side of the french doors and motioned him in. "Enjoy your dinner," she murmured as he walked past her.

"Thanks."

There were about fifteen adults in the room. They

were standing around in groups. Some had wine glasses in their hands. Others were eating hors d'oeuvres. In addition, Olivia and a smaller girl were sitting coloring at a small table in the corner. Michael stood watching them.

Aside from Kat and Bill, Glynnis, her brother and his wife, Dan knew none of the adults. But they all seemed to know him.

"Here he is," Glynnis said, hurrying over to his side. She looked beautiful, totally different from the woman he'd last seen on Wednesday. Tonight her hazel eyes—which looked almost green—were sparkling with happiness. Her shining red-gold hair was a mass of curls held back by gold combs, and she wore a beautiful deep green dress made out of some kind of shiny material.

Dan wasn't sure if it was taffeta or something else—he was no expert on women's fashions—but whatever it was, it complemented her eyes and hair and skin. Little diamond earrings glittered in her ears. Come to think of it, everything about her glittered tonight.

Glynnis tucked her hand under his arm. Happiness radiated from her. She smiled up at him, and their eyes met. He felt a completely unexpected jolt at the contact. Until that moment, he'd honestly believed his interest in her was more one of sympathy for her situation, but now he realized he'd been attracted to her all along. The attraction had simply been masked by his need to focus on finding her daughter.

"Come and meet my family and friends," she said. "Everyone, this is Kat's brother, the man of the hour—Lieutenant Dan O'Neill. He's my hero and our guest of honor."

Dan blinked at the "guest of honor" designation. She hadn't told him that when she'd asked him to come. If she had, he might have begged off.

Leading him forward, she introduced the other guests one by one. "This is my cousin Steve Antonelli—he's the assistant manager here—and his wife, Maggie, who's one of our chefs." A good-looking young couple—him, tall and on the fair side; her, small and dark and very pregnant—smiled and greeted him.

"We're all really grateful," Steve Antonelli said, giving him a firm handshake.

"Yes," echoed Maggie. "Can I give you a hug?"

Dan knew nothing he said was going to change anyone's mind about his role in Olivia's return, so he figured he might as well go with the flow and not try to contradict their impression that he had single-handedly rescued Glynnis's daughter. Wryly, he wondered how they'd feel if they knew the truth about him.

Just then, Gregg walked up and handed Dan a glass of red wine. "Our best Chianti," he said.

"Thanks." Dan took the wine. Rolled it around in the glass for a few moments, then sniffed, and took a taste. "Good."

"Hey, I'm impressed. He knows about wine," Gregg said.

"One of my few areas of expertise."

"Oh, I think you have more than a few," Gregg said. "My sister would say you're a Superman. We all would."

Dan wasn't sure he could stand much more praise. If these people only knew how far from being a Superman he really was, they'd be singing a different tune.

Gregg's gaze moved to the table where the two little girls were sitting. "Look at her. You'd never know anything had ever happened."

"Kids are resilient," Dan said, relieved to have the spotlight move from him to Olivia. "Plus, she was treated well."

"Glynnis tells me that Wilkerson woman's kid died last year, and that she's never gotten over it."

They talked a while longer about Tammy Wilkerson, and Dan answered questions about the actual recovery of Olivia.

"That's enough serious conversation," Glynnis finally said, tugging him away. "You haven't met everyone yet."

In short order, she introduced him to the remaining guests: a Scottish woman who taught at the college and her husband, a scholarly type who held an unlit pipe in his mouth; a cheerful middle-aged couple who Glynnis said were her next-door neighbors; Father Kelly, the pastor of Glynnis's church; a pretty blonde who looked about sixteen but who was the teacher of Olivia's class at her day care center; several women from the choir—it turned out Glynnis sang in her church choir; and a handsome fiftyish man Glynnis introduced as her boss, along with his attractive wife.

By now, Kat and Bill had joined the group milling around Dan. Bill gave Dan a friendly punch on the arm, the standard greeting with the O'Neill clan.

Dan liked Bill. He was a big, warm, friendly bear of a guy—a good husband to Kat and a great father to his two boys.

"How's it feel to be a hero?" Bill said, grinning.

"Don't you start," Dan warned.

Bill just laughed.

Kat gave Dan a kiss. "Have I told you lately that I think you're great?" she murmured.

"It's about time," he deadpanned.

Now it was her turn to punch him playfully. "Don't push your luck."

"Okay, everyone, it's time to eat. Let's all find our seats," Gregg said.

Finding his place card, Dan realized he'd been given the place of honor at Glynnis's right. He just hoped the thank-yous had finally been exhausted and the rest of the evening would focus on someone other than him. He soon saw that wish was futile, because once everyone was seated, two waiters filled champagne flutes for the adults and the children were given sparkling grape juice. When they'd finished, Gregg, who sat at the foot of the table, stood to propose a toast. "To Dan," he said.

Dan shot him a look.

"And to the rest of the Ivy Police Department," Gregg added.

Everyone drank and cheered.

"Speech, speech," Gregg's wife called out.

Dan could have cheerfully strangled her. He had no choice but to get to his feet. "I'm not the kind of guy who can give clever speeches," he began.

"That's true," Kat said. "Unless he's lecturing one of his siblings."

Everyone laughed.

"I just want to say I'm happy I had the good luck to be the one who got the call that ended this story happily." His gaze met Glynnis's, and she gave him a warm smile. "Sometimes that doesn't happen." An image he had tried to bury swam into his vision. "That's why I feel uncomfortable when people thank me for times when things go well."

Dan was saved from having to think of anything further by the entrance of several waiters.

Gregg's chef had outdone himself. The meal started with antipasto served on large platters. Dan took a liberal helping of the thinly sliced salami, proscuitto and cheese, as well as a generous portion of the marinated peppers, olives, artichoke hearts, tomatoes and eggplant.

Next came a delicious, richly flavored minestrone soup accompanied by crusty Italian bread.

After the soup, platters of pasta were served. The guests were encouraged to sample some of each: fet-

tucine Alfredo, ravioli with marinara sauce or gnocci with a mouth-watering marsala mushroom sauce.

By the time the main course—osso bucco and roasted asparagus—was served, Dan wasn't sure he could eat another bite.

"Save room for dessert," Glynnis warned. "It's the house specialty—Italian cream cake."

Dan moaned along with the other guests. But he managed to eat some of the osso bucco and the cake.

Glynnis was a terrific hostess, he thought. In fact, it was hard to reconcile this vibrant, confident woman with the pale, frightened woman he'd come to know over the course of the investigation that led to Olivia's safe return. He enjoyed talking to her, but he particularly enjoyed watching her relate to the other guests.

She never seemed ill at ease or lacking for something to say. Dan had never been good at small talk, especially not with strangers, and Glynnis seemed to sense that. When her boss asked Dan what had brought him back to Ivy, and Dan hesitated, she smiled and said, "I'm just grateful he's here," and Dan was saved from having to formulate some lie.

"I'm so glad you could come tonight," Glynnis said over coffee.

"It's been fun, and the food was incredible."

She smiled proudly. "Gregg's done a marvelous job here. Of course, he has a great chef."

Almost as if he'd heard her praise, the chef made an entrance. Dan was surprised at how young he seemed. Gregg introduced him around, and everyone complimented him on the great food.

After that, the guests began to stir and get ready to leave. As they said goodbye to Glynnis, he admired the way she found something personal to say to each guest.

When it was Dan's turn to say goodbye, he thanked her for asking him. "I had a great time."

"I'm glad."

"Um." He shifted awkwardly. "Would you mind if I dropped in once in a while to see how Olivia's doing?"

"Mind? I'd love it. Anytime. You're always welcome."

The warmth of her smile stayed with him all the way home. But still, he couldn't help wondering: was that really a promise he'd glimpsed in her eyes, or merely gratitude?

Glynnis hoped Dan had been telling the truth when he'd said he'd enjoyed himself tonight. Certainly everyone had made a fuss over him. He was definitely the hero of the hour.

She couldn't get over how different he'd been tonight. All the other times she'd been around him, he'd been on the job and all business. Tonight, he seemed younger, more boyish and vulnerable, even tongue-tied at times. Perhaps he was simply embarrassed by the attention and praise, as he'd suggested.

He certainly was good-looking. How was it she hadn't noticed that before? Even as she asked herself the question, she realized it was foolish. She hadn't noticed much of anything before. All she'd been able to think about was Olivia and whether she'd ever see her again.

Thanks to Dan, this story had a happy ending. Even if she hadn't liked him and even if he hadn't been Kat's brother, she'd want him to be her friend and remain a part of their lives, so she was thrilled when he mentioned that he'd like to stop by occasionally.

"Tonight was fun, wasn't it?" Sabrina said, breaking into Glynnis's thoughts.

The two, along with their three children, were riding home together. Gregg would stay on at the restaurant until closing.

"Yes, it was."

"I really like Dan O'Neill."

Glynnis smiled. "I think everyone did."

"Gregg said he used to work for the Chicago PD."

"Yes, that's what Kat told me."

"Why'd he want to come to Ivy after working somewhere like that?"

"Kat said he was on the vice squad. That's a pretty tough job, I'd guess. Maybe he just got burned out. Or maybe he wanted to be closer to his family."

"Well, whatever the reason, I'm glad he's here."

"Yes, me too."

Sabrina glanced into the back seat. "The kids have all fallen asleep." Her voice softened. "They look so sweet."

Glynnis flipped on her right turn signal.

"I think he likes you," Sabrina said.

"What? Who?"

"Don't play dumb. You know who. The handsome detective who rescued your daughter."

Glynnis knew her cheeks were warm. She was glad the car interior was dark so Sabrina wouldn't know she was blushing. "Well, I hope he likes me. I wouldn't want him to *dislike* me."

"That's not what I meant, and you know it. I think he's *interested* in you."

Glynnis shook her head, but even as she denied Sabrina's comment, she couldn't help feeling a spark of excitement. She knew she wasn't ready for a romantic relationship, not even close, but still…it was nice to think a good-looking guy like Dan might find her attractive. After all, she was only human.

Yet the more she thought about it, the more she realized how foolhardy it would be to encourage him. For one thing, even if he *were* interested in her, his interest wouldn't last long, not once he learned what a mess she'd made of her life in the past. So if she allowed herself to hope for more, she was going to get hurt. Again.

She wasn't ready to take another chance. And even if she had been, there were the children to think of. It wasn't even two years since Ben had died. Michael was only now beginning to adjust to his absence in their lives. Livvy, thank God, had been too young to have Ben's death affect her much.

Right now, and for the foreseeable future, Glynnis needed to focus on her kids and her career. Get her life together and learn to depend on herself and herself alone.

Learn to forgive myself...

Yes, that, too, she thought sadly.

Only then would she be ready for the kind of relationship she wanted. The kind of relationship that would last and grow.

Whether that relationship would be with Dan, only time would tell. In the meantime, they would have to remain just friends.

Chapter Six

Dan was on call Christmas Day, but he didn't have to go into the station. He slept in because he'd gone to Midnight Mass the night before along with his parents and his youngest sister, Renny, and her fiancé.

It was his first Midnight Mass in years, and even though he'd been reluctant, afterwards he was glad he'd gone. He enjoyed the service, and he especially enjoyed knowing he'd made his mother happy. And she was happy. She kept smiling at him, and her eyes shone with pride when she introduced him to some of her friends after mass.

For years, Kat had teased Dan about being the favorite son. He'd always scoffed or turned her comments into a joke, saying things like, "What's the matter, you jealous?" But down deep, he knew it was true. He *was* his mother's favorite. On his darkest days, he believed his mother felt sorry for him because he'd made such a poor choice in a wife and because he'd lost his child. In more reasonable moments, he knew everyone made mistakes. The thing about mistakes was, a person should learn from them and not repeat them, something he was trying hard to remember.

Today, the entire O'Neill clan would be gathering at the family home for dinner. Until then, Dan had several hours free.

After eating his usual bowl of Cheerios and bananas, he showered and dressed in dark gabardine slacks and a white turtleneck sweater, then he loaded all the presents he'd bought into several large shopping bags. Three of the gaily wrapped packages he placed on the front seat of his car. They were gifts for Glynnis and her children.

At first, he'd hesitated, wondering if buying something for them was a bad idea. Then he'd thought, why not? They'd all been through a rough time, and because of his role in what had happened, they had become important in his life. Plus, he liked them. He liked them a lot. So he'd gone ahead and followed his instincts. He hoped they'd get as much pleasure from the gifts as he'd gotten from choosing them.

About noon he headed for Glynnis's house. He hadn't called ahead—he preferred the element of surprise—so he had no idea if she and the children were home or not. If they weren't, he'd call Glynnis tomorrow and stop by then.

The house looked nice. He saw that she'd put lights on the big blue spruce in front the way he'd imagined she might. Colored lights from the tree inside shone through the picture window, and a huge wreath with red velvet ribbon and gold pinecones hung on the front door. All the scene needed to turn it into a Currier and Ives print was snow, but after that first snowfall the day he'd found Olivia, the area hadn't had another. It was awfully cold, though. The temperatures had been below freezing for three days now, and the weather forecasters were predicting snow for the weekend.

Juggling his packages, he rang the doorbell. Through the glass side panels, he could see Glynnis coming down the hall. When the door opened, he grinned. "Merry Christmas!"

"Dan!" Her face lit up in a smile. "Merry Christmas to you, too. What are you doing here?"

He could see Michael peeking shyly around her. "I ordered a few things from Santa that I wanted to bring you." He winked at Michael, not sure if he still believed in Santa or not. Seven-year-olds were pretty world-wise nowadays.

Michael grinned. Dan's gaze met Glynnis's again.

"You didn't have to do this," she murmured as she stood aside to let him in.

By now Livvy had run into the hall. She looked cute enough to take a chunk out of, in a red-and-green plaid dress and green tights. Her bright hair was caught up with a green satin bow. The effect wasn't quite what he imagined Glynnis had envisioned, because jelly was smeared on Livvy's face and he could see that some had spilled onto her dress. Plus, she was wearing only one patent leather shoe. He smothered a chuckle.

"Oh, Livvy!" Glynnis said. "Honestly. Didn't I tell you to keep that bib on while you were eating? And where's your other shoe?" To Dan, she said sotto voce, "This child is going to give me gray hairs before my time. She doesn't hear anything she doesn't want to hear."

Livvy looked down at her feet. "My shoe's inda kitchen."

Glynnis rolled her eyes, and now Dan could no longer hold back the laughter.

"Michael," Glynnis said, "why don't you take Lieutenant O'Neill into the living room, while I go out to the kitchen and get your sister cleaned up, okay?" Looking at Dan, she added, "We'll join you in a minute. While I'm out there, what can I get you? Would you like some coffee? I've got a fresh pot. Or some eggnog? I've also got Coke and root beer if you'd rather have a soft drink."

"A glass of root beer sounds great."

She took Livvy's hand and they headed for the kitchen, while Dan followed Michael into the living room. Dan whistled when he saw the presents spread around the room. "Looks like Santa left half his bag here last night."

"Wanna see what I got?" Michael asked.

"Sure."

Michael proceeded to show off his loot: a scooter ("I wanted this the most!"), a pair of ice skates ("As soon as the pond freezes, Mom said she'll take us skating."), a new computer game ("Do you like to play computer games?"), two new games for his Game Boy, several articles of clothing, a puzzle, a Harry Potter book ("My mom's gonna help me read it 'cause it's pretty hard."), a CD and a video.

"Boy," Dan said, "you made out like a bandit, didn't you?"

Michael grinned. "Livvy got lots of cool stuff, too."

"I can see that." Dan looked around at the dolls, the pink baby carriage, the play dishes, the pretend stove, the mound of clothes, the red tricycle. He also saw a small pair of ice skates that were obviously hers. "You kids sure are lucky."

Michael nodded seriously. "My mom said tomorrow we're gonna go through our toy boxes and take out everything we haven't played with this year and then we're gonna give those things to kids that don't get much for Christmas." Michael frowned. "I don't know why Santa doesn't give everybody lots of stuff."

Dan was glad to see Glynnis was trying to teach her kids to be grateful for what they had and to realize not everyone was as fortunate. His mother had always done the same thing, even though there were seven of them and when finances were really tight they'd been lucky to get anything. Still, the O'Neill clan had always had a roof over their heads, plenty to eat and decent clothes to wear. A lot more than many people. "I think parents have to help Santa out."

"Oh, you mean, like, give him money?"

Dan nodded. "I think so. What does your mother say about it?"

Michael lifted his shoulders. "She just said some kids don't get much, and it's important that we share what we have."

"Well, I think she's right."

"Santa brought my mom some new paints and stuff. She's an artist." This last was said proudly.

"Is she?" Dan knew Glynnis taught art at the community college, so he wasn't surprised. For the first time, he paid attention to the paintings on the walls. There were three of them in the living room—a large painting over the fireplace, and two smaller ones on the far wall. All were abstract and wildly colorful. Dan didn't know anything about art, so he wasn't sure if there was a name for the style or not. He wondered if Glynnis had painted them. He made a mental note to ask her about them.

While he'd been studying the paintings, Michael had pulled the scooter out from behind the tree. "Wanna see me ride my scooter?"

"Wait a minute, young man. What did I tell you about riding it in the house?" Glynnis had walked in before Michael finished his question. She handed Dan a frosty mug filled with root beer.

"Thanks." Olivia wasn't the only one who looked pretty today, he thought. So did Glynnis, who was dressed in tan slacks, a gold sweater with sparkly beads around the neckline and bottom, and dangling gold earrings. What a difference a week had made.

"I didn't mean in the house, Mom," Michael said with an exasperated, grownups-are-so-silly expression on his face.

"Well, excuse me," Glynnis said. Her eyes were filled with laughter as they met Dan's.

Dan bit back a grin. "Tell you what. When I get ready to leave, you can come out and show me then. If that's all right with your mother."

"Can I, Mom?"

"We'll see."

Michael looked as if he was going to protest, but then he just sighed and said, "Okay."

"In the meantime, I've got some presents for you," Dan said. He handed Michael his, then passed Glynnis's and Olivia's on to Glynnis.

Michael squealed when he found a baseball glove in his box. "Cool! Look, Mom! A baseball glove just like the Indians use."

"His favorite team is the Indians," Glynnis said.

"Isn't everyone's?" Dan said.

"Thank you, Lieutenant O'Neill," Michael said. He pronounced Dan's title "tenant."

"That's kind of a mouthful. Why don't you call me Dan?"

Michael shot a look at his mother.

She hesitated. "I really don't like for the kids to call adults by their first names."

"Lieutenant O'Neill is pretty tough for a kid to say," Dan pointed out.

"Well…" She smiled. "This one time, I guess it's all right."

Dan looked at Michael. "Anyway, you're welcome, Michael. I'm glad you like the glove."

"Maybe Uncle Gregg will come and play catch with me," Michael said.

"I'm sure he will," Glynnis said.

"I'd be happy to come and work out with you, too," Dan said impulsively.

"You *would?*" Michael said. *"Cool!"*

Once again, Dan met Glynnis's gaze. For a moment, he was afraid he had overstepped the boundaries of their budding friendship, but when, after a moment, she smiled, he realized she was pleased by his offer, even if it had surprised her.

He also realized how much he wanted to see her smiles and how much he liked being the one to put them there. Maybe it *wasn't* just gratitude she felt toward him. Maybe he had a chance for something more.

By now, Olivia had torn the wrapping off her present and had lifted out the white stuffed polar bear Dan hadn't been able to resist buying. "Bear!" she shouted, hugging the animal. She raced over to his side and hugged his legs.

Impulsively, Dan picked her up and put her on his lap for a moment. Holding her, feeling her warmth, smelling the little-girl scent of her skin and hair, Dan's pleasure was bittersweet. Although Livvy looked nothing like Mona, who had been blond and blue-eyed like her mother, every time he was around her he was reminded of something Mona had said or done when she'd been Livvy's age.

"Bear, Mommy!" Olivia held the bear out toward her mother.

"I know. And what do you say to Dan, sweetie?" Glynnis prompted.

"Tank you!" Livvy kissed the bear, then wiggled to be released. "My bear," she said possessively when Dan set her down again.

Glynnis shook her head, saying in a soft aside to Dan, "She's very territorial right now."

Dan grinned.

Now it was Glynnis's turn to open her gift. Dan had spent a long time deciding on something to give her. He knew it shouldn't be too personal, but he didn't want to give her something totally impersonal, like a book, either. He hoped she would like what he'd finally chosen.

"Oh," she breathed when she lifted the gift out of its nest of tissue paper. She stroked the inlaid wood of the small box, slowly lifting its cover. The inside was lined with red velvet, and as they listened, the tinkling notes of "Somewhere Over the Rainbow" began to play. "Oh, it's lovely, Dan. Thank you so much, but…"

"But what?"

"You shouldn't have."

"I couldn't come with presents for the kids and not for you, could I? Besides, isn't Christmas a time for giving?"

"Well, when you put it that way…"

"I do. Anyway, I'm glad you like it. I thought, you know, you could keep jewelry in it."

"It's perfect for jewelry. I love it. It's just beautiful."

"Mine!" Olivia said, reaching for the box.

"No, sweetie, this is Mommy's."

Livvy frowned. "Mine," she said again.

Glynnis gave Dan an amused look. "I'm afraid we've created a monster. She thinks everything is hers." Turning back to her daughter, she said more firmly, "Not every present is yours, Livvy. This is Mommy's present. How would you like it if I tried to take your bear away from you?" She reached toward the bear.

"No! My bear!" Livvy said, holding the bear away and giving her mother an outraged look.

"That's right. That's your bear, and this is my music box." Glynnis carefully set the box on a nearby table, then went to the tree. Bending down, she removed a narrow wrapped package. "We have something for you, too, Dan." She handed the box to him.

Dan didn't know what to say. He'd never expected anything from Glynnis, wasn't even sure if it was appropriate for him to receive a gift. What if it was viewed as some kind of payment from her? But he knew it would hurt her feelings if he refused, so he took the box and slowly opened it.

Inside was a soft, charcoal gray scarf. Feeling it, he suspected it was cashmere. "Wow. This is nice." He smiled at Glynnis. "I don't have a decent scarf anymore. I left the one I had somewhere and haven't bothered to buy another."

"I noticed you didn't have one on the night of the party," she said softly. "So I thought…anyway, I'm glad you like it."

"I do. I like it very much. Thank you." Because he felt awkward now, he changed the subject. "I noticed both of the kids got skates for Christmas. Do you like to skate?"

"I love it. We all do."

"Where do you go?"

"The pond at Whitney Park. Do you know it?"

"Sure. We skated there when I was a kid."

"It's not frozen yet, but another couple of days of temperatures like this, and it will be. Then we'll go."

"Yay," Michael said.

Dan thought about his old pair of ice skates. He still had them, even though he hadn't skated in years. Not since before Mona got sick. Since then, the skates had been packed up in a box, and when he'd moved, they'd come along.

"Kat and Bill and the kids go skating all the time," Glynnis continued.

"Do they? I'll have to tag along sometime." He

hesitated, then added casually, "Maybe we can all go together."

"That would be fun."

"I'll talk to Kat about it today."

"You're all getting together at your parents'?"

"Yeah. The whole clan will be there."

"Really? All your brothers and sisters?"

"Except for Tim and his family."

"Tim's the one who lives in Phoenix?"

"Yes."

"He's an engineer, right?"

"Computer software specialist."

"I can't keep them straight."

He grinned. "Sometimes I can't, either."

"You're so lucky to have a big family." Her tone was wistful. "I'll bet having everyone there makes your mother happy."

"She'll be over the moon."

Glynnis smiled. "We're going over to Gregg's in a little while." She glanced at her watch. "Very soon, as a matter of fact."

"I'd better leave then, so you can get ready."

As they said goodbye, they shook hands. Dan knew it was too soon to even think about kissing her, but knowing something and doing it were two different things, because in that moment—looking down into her beautiful, gold-flecked eyes—he wanted to kiss her more than he'd wanted anything in a long time.

It might just be wishful thinking, but there was

something about her expression that made him think maybe that's what she wanted, too.

"Aunt Sabina, looka what I got!"

Sabrina bent down to give Livvy a kiss. "That's sure a pretty doll. Did Santa bring you that?"

"Uh-huh," Livvy said, nodding vigorously.

"And look at this bear!" Sabrina said. "Isn't he the cutest?" She looked at Glynnis over Olivia's head, mouthing, *Where did you find this? I want one for Samantha.*

"The bear was a present from Dan O'Neill," Glynnis said.

"Really?"

"Yeah," Michael chimed in, "and he gave me a baseball glove. I brought it with me so me and Uncle Gregg can throw some balls later. And he gave my mom this box that plays music."

"Oh, *really?*" Sabrina said again. The expression on her face was speculative.

Glynnis knew what her sister-in-law was thinking and wished she could have been the one to mention the gifts in a more casual way.

"Merry Christmas, sis," Gregg said. He stood in the doorway to the kitchen. "I'll be there in a minute. Right now I'm basting the turkey."

Glynnis looked at Sabrina. "You sure have got him trained right."

"Hey, he's the food expert in this family. Why shouldn't he do most of the cooking?"

Gregg grinned and went back to the kitchen.

Later, after they'd exchanged their gifts and plied Gregg with praise for his wonderful dinner, Glynnis, Gregg and Sabrina sat over coffee in the family room while the children played happily nearby.

"So when did you see Dan to exchange presents?" Sabrina asked. "You *did* give him something, didn't you?"

"Yes, we gave him that scarf I told you about. Um, he dropped by earlier today."

"Oh, really?"

"I wish you'd quit saying *oh, really* like that."

"Oh, really?" Then Sabrina laughed. "Sorry. Couldn't resist."

"Is this an inside joke?" Gregg asked. "'Cause I don't know what you two are talking about."

"Dan O'Neill gave very nice Christmas presents to both Glynnis and the children. And what we're talking about is my observation—which I told Glynnis about the night of the party—that I think he's interested in her."

"He is not!" Glynnis said, realizing as soon as the words were out of her mouth that she was protesting too loudly.

Sabrina grinned. "Notice how she blushes every time I mention his name?"

"I do not!"

"Quit teasing her," Gregg said. But his gaze, as it met Glynnis's, was thoughtful. "I think maybe Sabrina's right, sis."

Oh, she wished they'd quit talking about this. She knew she really *was* blushing now. Why did she have to be a redhead with a complexion that let her have no secrets from anyone?

"What do you think of him?" Gregg continued.

"I think he's a wonderful person," Glynnis said. "After all, he found Olivia."

"We all think that. I meant personally. Because if you don't want him hanging around, I can talk to him."

Glynnis nearly choked on her coffee. "Don't you dare say one word to him."

"So you're interested?"

"I didn't say that, Gregg. I just meant I don't want you making an issue of this. Oh, my God, I'd be too embarrassed to even look him in the eye if you said anything."

Gregg grinned and said to Sabrina, "I think she wants us to mind our own business."

"You read my mind."

After that, the subject was dropped. But Glynnis kept thinking about what Gregg and Sabrina had said. She kept remembering the look in Dan's eyes as they'd said goodbye earlier. She'd have bet money that he wanted to kiss her. And she'd wanted him to. She'd wanted him to very much. So much for making sensible decisions, she thought wryly. Hardly a week had passed since she'd decided all she wanted from Dan O'Neill was friendship, and here she was thinking about kissing him.

What would have happened if he had? What would she have done? She was afraid she would have returned his kiss, because she'd never been much good at denying her feelings.

If she couldn't control herself, maybe it would be best if she didn't see Dan again. Her heart sank at the prospect. She told herself it was because she couldn't bear the idea of hurting his feelings.

But was that the only reason?

Be honest with yourself, Glynnis. You don't want to push him out of your life, no matter what the consequences. But for once, don't be impulsive. Think.

And yet…what if she and Gregg and Sabrina were all wrong about his supposed interest in her? Maybe they'd all misread what was simply friendliness on his part. After what he'd done for her, it would be awful if she turned away that friendship. It would be unconscionable.

Okay, so she'd have to walk a fine line. Let him know she valued his friendship, but if he *did* act as if he wanted more, somehow gently let him down so that he wouldn't feel rejected.

Even as she decided on her course of action, she knew it might not work. Because—when and if the time came—she might not be strong enough to say no.

When almost a week had gone by without Glynnis hearing from Dan, she told herself she was glad. Things had worked out for the best.

Today was New Year's Eve, and she'd been invited to share Sabrina's sitter and spend the evening with Sabrina and Gregg at the restaurant. That afternoon, she was standing looking into her closet and trying to decide what to wear for the night's festivities when the phone rang....

"Glynnis? Hi. It's Dan."

Her traitorous heart gave a glad little leap. "Hi."

"I've been meaning to call you for days, but things have been kind of crazy here at the station. We've got a bunch of guys on vacation, so I've been working some double shifts to help out."

"That's nice of you."

"Well, I don't have a family like they do, so it's not that big a deal for me. Plus, I get paid overtime. Listen, the reason I called is, I was wondering if you have plans for tomorrow."

"Tomorrow?"

"During the day. This morning I checked, and the pond at Whitney Park is frozen solid now. In fact, when I was there, there were a bunch of kids skating. I thought maybe you and the kids would like to go."

Make an excuse. Tell him a fib. Say Olivia has a cold and you don't want her outdoors for any length of time. "Th-that sounds like lots of fun. Sure, we'd love to go."

"Great. How about if I pick you up around one?"

"We'll be ready."

When they hung up, Glynnis sat on the bed. What

was *wrong* with her? Couldn't she stick to a decision? And yet, what was so bad about going skating in the afternoon with the kids along? It was a perfect way to spend time with Dan yet still keep to her resolution of friendship only.

And she knew the kids would be excited. They loved to skate, and they were both crazy about Dan.

Uh-huh. Tell me another one....

Ignoring her sarcastic conscience, she went looking for the kids. She could hardly wait to tell them about tomorrow. She was halfway to the playroom where they were watching a video when she realized it might not be such a good idea to broadcast her plans. Knowing the children, they'd be sure to mention something in Sabrina's hearing. And that was the last thing Glynnis needed.

Chapter Seven

It took Dan a while to find his skating legs. Glynnis and Michael looked like pros compared to him and Livvy. But one thing about Livvy—no matter how many times she fell, and she fell a lot at first, she'd pick herself right up and try again.

Dan, on the other hand, was a wimp. After his second fall, he wished he could just go sit on one of the benches and watch. But there was no way he'd let a three-year-old show him up.

He was glad when Glynnis decided she was tired and needed to rest a bit. Then he had an excuse to sit with her and watch the kids for a while.

"It's nice out here, isn't it?" she said.

"Yes, it is." Today the sun shone brightly overhead, which made the ice on the pond and the sprinkling of snow and ice on the trees sparkle. The colors of the coats and hats and scarves of the twenty or so skaters out today made a bright contrast against the winter landscape.

"I love winter," she said. "I'd miss it if I lived somewhere where it didn't snow."

"Me, too."

"I don't like driving when it's icy, though." She sighed. "Which reminds me of something I've been trying to forget—I go back to work Wednesday."

"Does the spring semester start that early?"

"No. The kids won't be back until next week. Teachers have to go early."

"You like teaching, though, don't you?"

She smiled. "Yes, I do. Not all the time, mind you. And I certainly don't like the politics. But I love working with the kids. Except for art history, the classes I teach are ones the kids want to take, so they're interested and eager to learn what I can teach them."

"Why is art history different?"

"To some students, it's boring. They only take it because it's required if you're an art major."

They were still talking about her job when someone tapped Dan's shoulder from behind. Turning around he saw his nephew Jonah—Kat's freckle-faced youngest—smiling at him.

"Hi, Uncle Dan. Hi, Mrs. March."

"Hey, Jonah," Dan said. "Did you just get here?"

"Uh-huh."

Dan looked beyond him, but didn't see Kat or Bill. "Who'd you come with?"

"I'm here with Ryan." He inclined his head toward a tall, thin blond boy who stood a little ways away. "He's my best friend."

Dan smiled at the boy, who gave him a shy smile back. "Well, you two boys have fun."

"We will," Jonah called as he and Ryan headed out onto the ice. They stopped when they reached the place where Michael and Livvy were skating. When Livvy fell again, Jonah immediately reached for her to help her up.

"What a nice kid he is," Glynnis said. "Most boys his age wouldn't want anything to do with children as young as Michael and Olivia."

"Yeah, Kat and Bill have done a good job with their boys." He turned to meet her gaze. "You're doing a good job with your kids, too."

"Thank you. They *are* good kids. I'm lucky."

"I don't think luck has much to do with it. Parenting is hard work." As soon as the words were out of his mouth, he wished he had phrased the comment another way, because he did not want to talk about Mona. The last thing he wanted was *Glynnis* feeling sorry for him, too. He'd had enough of that with his family and former co-workers.

"Harder even than I'd ever imagined. Especially when you're a single parent."

Yes, he knew all about being a single parent. It was damned hard. Those years after Cindy ran out on them had been tough. That was one of the reasons he admired Glynnis. She'd overcome a lot of adversity and didn't seem to feel sorry for herself.

"But it's worth it," she said. "I love my kids more than life itself." She gave an embarrassed laugh. "That sounds corny, doesn't it?"

"I don't think it sounds corny at all."

Dan almost spilled his guts right then and there. The temptation to tell her about Mona was strong, because he knew she'd understand exactly how he felt. If he could have, he would have exchanged places with Mona in a heartbeat. Watching her suffer had been the hardest thing he'd ever had to endure because he'd been completely helpless to do anything to make the pain go away.

That last month had been especially rough. He'd had to fight against giving in to the rage he felt about the atrocity of a child going through what Mona went through. Yet he knew letting Mona see his anger would only add to her burden, so he'd kept his feelings hidden and the only emotion he'd allowed her to see was the overwhelming love he felt for her.

After her death, the anger was gone. What was left was numbness. For days, he wandered around, barely able to function. He couldn't eat, he couldn't sleep, he couldn't concentrate. Sometimes he'd find himself somewhere and never remember how he'd gotten there.

The only reality was Mona's absence. He missed her so acutely, he wasn't sure he wanted to go on living without her. Yet somehow he had. And somehow he'd survived. But he'd never been the same. Loving Mona and losing her had changed him. The old Dan was gone, and the new Dan had to find a way to live a meaningful life without her.

Gradually, the pain eased, but even after nine years, the old sadness and depression could attack without warning. Today, it threatened, and Dan knew talking about Mona to Glynnis wasn't a good idea.

So he said nothing. And when, a few minutes later, Michael and Livvy skated over to say they were cold, and Glynnis said she thought it was time to leave, Dan was glad he hadn't put a pall on the day by crying on her shoulder.

When they reached her house, she smiled at him and said, "Want to come in for a cup of hot chocolate and a sandwich or something?"

Afterwards, Dan never knew where the strength to say no had come from, because there was nothing he would have liked more. But the discussion about children and parenting had left him raw, and the memories were fighting to take hold.

At times like this, Dan needed to be alone. He wasn't fit company for anyone, least of all Glynnis.

So he said, "Thanks, but I promised the chief I'd check in at the station by five."

"Oh, okay."

He heard the disappointment she tried to cover up. "Can I have a rain check?"

Now she smiled. "Of course."

He waited until she and the children were safely inside before walking back to his car.

Then he headed home to deal with his demons.

Glynnis found it even more difficult than she'd thought it would be to return to work, not just because she'd been off so long, but because it still made her uneasy to leave Olivia. She knew she was being overly protective but after what had happened, she didn't want to take any chances.

But she had to work. Even if she'd been willing to use any of the money Ben had left the children, it wouldn't last forever if she wasn't bringing in any income.

And she wasn't willing to use the money. That money was the children's inheritance.

Assuring herself the children would be fine—Michael in his school and Olivia in hers—Glynnis headed for the college. The first week wasn't as hard as she'd thought it would be. Both Michael and Olivia were filled with excitement at the end of each day, and gradually Glynnis relaxed.

The first day the students were back in class was another story. They had a hard time settling into study/work mode, too. Just as anticipated, art history classes were the toughest, but at least Glynnis had a late lunch with Kat to look forward to, and that helped her get through the sessions.

Glynnis was late arriving at Bootsie's, a popular soup, sandwich and salad place near the college. A student had kept her after class, but Kat said she hadn't been waiting long.

"I'm glad you suggested lunch today," Glynnis said, sitting and pulling off her gloves. She shrugged out of her coat and scarf and draped them over the back of her chair. After the freezing wind outside, the restaurant seemed overly warm.

"Me, too," Kat said. "I've missed our lunches while the kids were out of school." She smiled. "I've missed *you*."

"Oh, yeah, sure. You were probably thinking about me the whole time you were away," Glynnis teased. "How *was* the trip?"

Kat and Bill had parked their boys with his sister and taken off the day after New Year's for their annual vacation alone, and Glynnis hadn't talked to her since she'd been back.

"Oh, Glynnis, Bermuda is beautiful. We had a wonderful time." Her smile was mischievous. "Acted just like newlyweds."

Glynnis couldn't help the spurt of envy. All anyone had to do was take one look at Kat's face to know there sat a completely satisfied woman. But she quickly banished the feeling. Just because Glynnis missed having someone to share her bed and her life didn't mean she begrudged Kat her happiness.

Still talking about the trip, they got in line and ordered their food—vegetable soup and a salad for Glynnis, a tuna sandwich and mushroom soup for Kat. Once their orders were placed, they got their drinks, then walked back to their table to wait for their numbers to be called.

Kat squeezed lemon into her tea, then tore open a packet of crackers. "So how was your New Year's Eve?"

"It was fun. What about yours?"

Kat shrugged. "Truthfully? The party was kind of boring. I don't know. I think I'm getting too old to stay up that late."

Glynnis laughed. "You'll never be too old."

Kat drank some of her tea. "So what have you been up to?"

"Oh, the usual. Catching up around the house. Enjoying doing things with the kids. Nothing special."

"Jonah said he saw you and the kids ice-skating with Dan New Year's Day." The remark was said casually. Almost too casually.

For some reason, Glynnis felt uncomfortable, which made her mad at herself. She had no reason to feel funny about being with Dan. "Yes. We had such a good time. Your brother is really nice, Kat."

"I think so." Kat ate a cracker.

"The kids thought he was so funny because when he first started out, he fell a couple of times. But then he got the hang of it again, and pretty soon he was whizzing around the pond just like a young kid."

Kat smiled.

"The children adore him. He has a real knack with kids."

Kat was silent for a long moment. When she

spoke, her voice was thoughtful. "I told you about his daughter Mona, didn't I?"

Glynnis blinked. "His daughter? I didn't know he had a daughter. Does she live with his ex?"

"No." Kat sighed deeply. "Mona died."

"Oh, *no!* I had no idea. Recently?"

Kat shook her head. "No. It's been nine years. It's really sad. She had brain cancer. She was only six years old when it took her."

"Oh, my God, that's awful." Glynnis immediately thought of Michael and Livvy.

"Yes, it was pretty awful. It tore Dan up. I honestly don't think he's ever gotten over it."

"How could he? It's the worst thing that could ever happen to a person." Suddenly Glynnis remembered how they'd talked about parenting the day at the pond. How she'd said it was hard, and he'd agreed. Oh, God. She wished she'd known. She'd have been more careful. On the heels of that thought, she remembered how quiet he'd been when he'd taken them home. How he'd refused her offer of hot chocolate and something to eat. He'd probably been upset. She'd probably reminded him of everything he had lost. She wondered if that was why he hadn't called since.

Kat nodded. "Yes, it is the worst thing."

"Is…is that what broke up his marriage?"

"No, the marriage was over long before that. His wife ran out on him and Mona when Mona was only two years old."

Glynnis couldn't imagine how any woman could run out on her child. Was she crazy? And leave a great guy like Dan? She *must* have been crazy. "What happened?"

Kat shrugged. "It was a bad match to begin with. They didn't have a thing in common except sex. Not that Dan ever said that, but I have eyes." Kat made a face. "None of us liked her. We tried, for Dan's sake, but it was obvious to all of us that it was never going to last. Dan's loyal, though. I'm not sure he ever would have asked Cindy for a divorce—at least as long as Mona needed her."

"It must have been really tough on him, being left with a baby and with the kind of job he had…"

"Yeah, but you know, in a way I think it was also a relief. He no longer had to pretend."

"Where is his ex-wife now?"

"Who knows? I don't think he's heard from her since she left."

Glynnis's mouth dropped open. "You mean she just completely *abandoned* her baby?"

"Yeah. Nice gal, huh?"

"I'm speechless. I mean, I can't even *imagine* abandoning a child like that." Glynnis swallowed. "It was hard enough…what I had to do…and I knew my baby was going to a good home."

Kat reached across the table and squeezed Glynnis's hand. "Oh, Glynnis, I'm sorry. I didn't bring this up to make you feel bad. The two situations aren't even remotely similar. I just thought, since you and Dan are becoming friends, that you should know some things."

But, in a way, the two situations *were* similar, and for the rest of the day, Glynnis kept thinking about what Kat had told her. Dan must despise his ex-wife for what she did. What would he say if he knew that Glynnis had walked away from *her* baby, too?

Dan finished typing up his report on the domestic he'd been called out on the previous day. The woman had refused to press charges, even though she was obviously scared of her live-in boyfriend and had the bruises to prove his brutality. She even denied they'd been fighting, said the neighbor who'd called in had been mistaken.

"We just had the TV too loud, that's all," she insisted, the boyfriend glowering behind her.

They'd tried talking to her. Romeo had distracted the suspected abuser and Dan had talked to the woman, but she wouldn't change her mind. In the end, he and Romeo had no choice but to leave.

Dan would never understand the misguided loyalty that so many abused women seemed to feel for their lovers and/or husbands. Was it fear of being alone that kept them from leaving them? Or fear of even worse beatings?

He thought of all the women he knew. His mother, for instance. In her seventies and from a much more traditional generation than the woman who'd gotten beaten up.

Brenda O'Neill, mother of seven, a woman who'd never held an outside job. Married to a strong-willed, physical man who ruled his household with an iron fist. Yet Dan's mother was spirited and strong-willed herself. She took no guff from anyone and especially not from Big Mike—as Dan's father had been nicknamed as a teenager. Anytime Big Mike got a little too loud or too controlling for her taste, she would knock him down a peg or two. A few well-placed words or that expression she got on her face, the one that said *If I were you, I wouldn't mess with me,* and Big Mike would be cowed.

Dan's sisters were pretty much the same—from Renny, the youngest, who was a pediatric resident at County General, to Shawn, the oldest, a social worker who had been the driving force behind the building of a new Assistance Ministries Center in the town in Connecticut where she and her husband lived—they were all strong, independent women who would never allow anyone to push them around or intimidate them.

His phone rang and, as if she'd known he was thinking about his sisters, he discovered Kat on the other end.

"I've got a pot of chili on. Why don't you come and have dinner with us? I'm making corn bread, too." As usual, Kat talked a mile a minute.

"Sounds good. What time?"

"What time do you get off work?"

"My shift is over at four."

"Come then."

"Don't *you* have to work today?"

"I have one appointment at eleven. A listing. Other than that, nothing. January's a slow time for the real estate market."

"Okay. I'll see you sometime after four, then. Want me to bring anything?"

"Just your handsome self."

Dan was smiling when he hung up. He always enjoyed being with Kat and her family.

Even though she'd said he didn't have to bring anything, once he was on his way, he decided to stop at Rosalie's Bakery and pick up one of her New York-style cheesecakes, which he knew was a particular favorite of his brother-in-law.

When he arrived at Kat's, he found her washing salad greens at the sink in the kitchen island. "Brought dessert," he said.

Her eyes lit up. "Rosalie's cheesecake! Bill will think he's died and gone to heaven. Thanks." She inclined her head. "Cold beer in the fridge."

After giving her a kiss on the cheek, Dan put the cheesecake in the refrigerator and helped himself to a beer. Then he pulled a bar stool up to the island so he could watch her.

"What's that thing?" he asked.

"This?" She grinned. "It's a salad spinner. See?" She demonstrated. "You put your washed lettuce leaves inside here, put the top on, then pump this gizmo. The leaves spin around inside, getting rid of the excess water. Presto. Clean and dry lettuce leaves."

"What won't they think of next?"

She laughed. "You're so out of it."

"Yeah, I know."

"Do you do *any* cooking at home, Dan?"

Dan thought about his apartment's miniscule kitchen. He thought about his sparsely filled cupboards and the fridge that contained beer, milk, apples and little else. "Does Cheerios with bananas count?"

She rolled her eyes. "What about dinner? Don't you ever fix a meal for yourself?"

"Not if I can help it."

"What do you eat?"

"Takeout. And if I feel like a home cooked meal—" he grinned "—I call Mom."

"Who's always happy to oblige her boys," Kat said drily.

"Do I detect a little sarcasm there?"

Chuckling, she finished spinning the lettuce and began to pull apart the dry pieces and put them in a big salad bowl. "I had lunch with Glynnis today."

"Oh?" He'd been thinking about Glynnis a lot lately, although he hadn't talked with her or seen her since the day they'd gone ice skating. It wasn't that he hadn't wanted to, just that he'd struggled with a recurrence of the depression that still occasionally dogged him, and he hadn't wanted to subject her to his black mood. Today was the first day he'd felt like fit company for anyone.

Kat was still talking. "I told her Jonah had mentioned seeing you ice-skating."

"Yeah, I took her and the kids New Year's Day. You should have seen Olivia on skates. She loved it!" He smiled thinking of how cute she'd been. "She's something else. No matter how many times she took a spill, she'd get up and try again. I don't think I've ever seen so much determination." Then he added, "Not since you were a kid, anyway."

"How would you know? You're only six years older."

"Maybe, but I remember how many times you fell learning to roller skate, and how you wouldn't give up."

Kat smiled. "I was a stubborn little cuss."

Dan raised his eyebrows. *"Was?"*

Now she laughed. "Okay, still am."

"Glad you admit it."

Kat was now cutting up baby carrots. "How'd the ice-skating come about?"

"What do you mean?"

"You know. Did she invite you to go with them, or did you ask her?"

"Why does it matter?"

"It doesn't. I was just curious."

"Okay, Kat, obviously you've got something on your mind. Why don't you just spill it?"

Kat dumped the cut up carrots into the salad bowl. Her eyes—astute O'Neill eyes—met his. "You're right. I guess I'm not the subtle sort. Now don't get mad, but it worries me that you're spending so much time with Glynnis and her children."

"*Worries* you? Why?"

Kat sighed. "Because you're my brother and you've had some rotten breaks. Because I don't want to see you get hurt again."

"Geez, Kat, don't make such a big deal out of this. I just took the woman and her kids ice-skating. Besides, I'm not *spending so much time with them,* as you put it. I haven't even seen Glynnis since New Year's Day. But even if I was, I'm a big boy. I can take care of myself."

"I knew you'd get mad if I said anything."

"I'm not mad." But he was. And he knew his expression showed it. "I don't understand you. I thought Glynnis was your best friend."

"She is. And I love her. But that doesn't stop me from seeing her clearly." She reached for one of the tomatoes sitting on the drainboard.

"What's that supposed to mean?"

"It means Glynnis looks like she's got it all together, but she doesn't. There are a lot of unresolved issues in her life, Dan. Some of them I'm not even at liberty to talk about, because she told me about them in confidence. But the bottom line is, I don't think she's ready for another relationship."

"Like I said before, I'm a big boy."

Kat began to cut up the tomato. "It's not just you I'm worried about. Glynnis is awfully vulnerable. I don't want her to get hurt, either."

"Hell, Kat, I don't want to see her get hurt, either. Anyway, I don't know what you're worried about. You're making a big deal out of nothing. Glynnis and I are just friends." *And that's probably all we'll ever be.*

She raised her eyebrows.

"We have a good time together. I like her, and I like her kids." Jesus, why was he explaining himself? Why didn't he just tell Kat this was none of her damned business?

Kat took a red onion out of the refrigerator. "Just think about what I've said, okay?"

Dan finished his beer and got up to throw the bottle into the trash.

"Want another?"

He shook his head. "Where're the boys?"

"Jonah had a clarinet lesson after school. He should be home any time. And Billy has hockey practice. Why? You trying to get away from me?"

He sat back down on the stool. "No, I'm not trying to get away from you." But he had been, and he could tell she knew it. What she'd said had bothered him, more even than he'd let on. And he wasn't bothered just by the fact that whether he spent time with Glynnis and her kids was his business and not Kat's.

What really bothered him was the thought that Kat might be right. That he might be letting himself in for more trouble than he could handle.

"I'm sorry, Dan," Kat said. "I should have kept my mouth shut about Glynnis."

"No, it's okay." For a moment, they were both silent, then he said, "How did you and Glynnis meet, anyway? I know she's older than you are."

"I was the real estate agent who sold her and Ben the house." She smiled. "She and I hit it off right away. I knew we were going to become friends, and we did." Covering the salad bowl with plastic wrap, she put it in the refrigerator. "She's probably the closest friend I've ever had." Meeting his eyes again, she said, "She's a wonderful person, Dan. She deserves happiness. I'm just—"

"I know. Don't say it. I got the message." To soften his words, he added, "And I *will* think about what you said."

Just then, the back door opened, and Bill walked in. The subject of Glynnis wasn't mentioned again.

Glynnis had been thinking about Dan all day. It had been ten days now, and she still hadn't heard from him. As she cleaned up the art room in preparation for her next class, she decided it would be perfectly okay for her to call him. After all, she reasoned, he had given her and the children a wonderful day of ice-skating, and the correct thing to do was repay him. Anyway, he *had* asked for a rain check when she'd invited him to stay for hot chocolate, hadn't he? Yes, he had. So she should definitely call him.

With what she wanted to do anyway justified, she decided she would make lasagna from her Grandmother Antonelli's recipe and invite him over.

He wasn't at the station, and his cell phone only yielded his voice mail, so she left a message. Later that afternoon, he returned her call.

"Glad I caught you," he said. "I got your message."

"I called to invite you to dinner Saturday night." When he didn't answer immediately, she hurriedly added, "If you're free, that is."

"I'm free."

Glynnis hadn't realized she'd been holding her breath until it was released. "Good. I hope you like lasagna."

"What red-blooded man doesn't like lasagna?"

Glynnis chuckled. "Good point. We eat kind of early. Do you mind?"

"As long as it's not before four. I'm on duty Saturday."

"Not *that* early. Why don't you come around five? We'll eat about six."

"Can I bring anything? A bottle of wine, maybe?"

"That would be great."

When the call was over, Glynnis sat there smiling. Nothing was wrong. She'd been silly to worry that she'd somehow offended him. Dan had probably just been busy. Gathering up the pop quiz papers she intended to grade that evening, she stuffed them into her satchel, put on her coat, scarf and gloves, and headed out the door for home.

It was only then she realized her day-end weariness was gone.

Chapter Eight

"Ready for some dessert?"

Dan patted his stomach. "After that dinner, I should say no." He and Glynnis were sitting in her kitchen over coffee. The kids were in bed, full of lasagna and tired from the day.

"I made lemon meringue pie."

Dan groaned.

"I take it that's a yes."

He grinned. "Just not too big a piece."

They didn't talk much as they ate their pie. In fact, she was silent so long, Dan began to feel uncomfortable. He scrambled for something to say. Finally he blurted out, "Kat's told me about your marriage."

She looked up. As he had been from the first day

he met her, he was struck by her eyes and the hint of sadness they contained.

"I figured she had." Glynnis put her fork down and pushed her plate away.

For some reason, the small piece of pie she'd left lying there looked forlorn and made Dan feel bad. "I'm sorry. I shouldn't have mentioned it."

"No, it's okay." She shrugged. "Shoot, everyone knows. It's not a secret."

"I respect how you don't seem angry about what happened."

"Don't give me too much credit. I've had my days when I've been furious with Ben." Her smile was wry. "In fact, there've been some days when if he'd been here, I'd have killed him myself."

"Who could blame you?"

"Me."

"What do you mean?"

Sighing, she fiddled with the spoon for her coffee. "The thing is, Dan, it takes two to conspire."

"I don't get what you're saying. He lied to you, didn't he? How did you conspire in that?"

"I just meant I was easy pickings. Maybe Ben didn't consciously know that, but he sensed it. Of all the women he could have met, I was a woman who was extremely susceptible to someone like him."

When she broke off, Dan waited patiently. It was obvious she wanted to talk, and he wanted to hear whatever it was she was willing to tell him.

Sighing again, she said, "It took me a while to figure this all out, but when I did it all made sense. I *wanted* him to be what I thought he was because I needed that from him. So I didn't question him when he said he worked for a variety of travel and tour companies as a freelancer. Or when he said he didn't work from an office but just had an answering service and I should call there if I needed him. Or when he said he would be traveling in a foreign country and might not be able to call me until he was back in the States. I never wondered why he had no friends. Why no one ever called him except occasionally on his cell phone. When he was home, he never wanted us to be with other people, and I told myself I was lucky that he loved me so much he didn't want to share me." She shook her head. "See what I mean? I was stupid. I saw what I wanted to see. Believed what I wanted to believe. I've done that my whole life. But I'm trying to change. I'm tired of making bad choices."

The censure in her voice bothered him. "Why are you so hard on yourself?"

She shrugged and looked away.

There was something so achingly vulnerable about the set of her shoulders. It made Dan want to get up and gather her into his arms and tell her no one would ever hurt her again. But he fought the impulse, not just because he wasn't sure how she'd react to that kind of attention from him but because, friends or not, he now reluctantly agreed with Kat.

It probably wasn't a wise idea to get too emotionally involved with Glynnis.

Even to his untrained eye, Glynnis had a lot of unresolved problems, problems he was ill-qualified to handle. Especially considering his own failures.

"I don't think I'm hard on myself," she said. "I'm just realistic."

"Everyone makes mistakes." He realized this was probably no more consolation to her than it had been to him.

"Yes, I know that," she said. "But other people actually seem to learn something from theirs. I'm like that commercial. You know the one, with the bunny. I just keep on going…and going and going… making one mistake after another."

"Look, if you're talking about what happened with Olivia, that was an accident. Something that could've happened to anyone."

"But it didn't happen to anyone," she said sadly. "It happened to me. And it happened because I was careless, which is a huge mistake and something a good parent can't afford to be."

"Glynnis, you're one of the best parents I know."

She swallowed and looked away, but not before he saw the gleam of tears in her eyes.

Unable to help himself, he reached over and clasped her hand. "C'mon, it's over. We found her. She's okay. Nothing bad happened. It's time to stop blaming yourself and move on."

When she didn't answer, he squeezed her hand.

"What good does it do anyone to keep beating your-self up over it? Geez, Glynnis, you're only human."

"You don't know…"

"But I *do* know."

She shook her head. "No. You *don't* know. I…" She closed her eyes. He could see she was wrestling with herself. "Olivia isn't the only daughter I've lost," she whispered.

"What?"

When her eyes opened and met his again, there was a bleakness there that tore at him.

"Only a few people know about this." She took a deep breath, and he could tell whatever it was she was going to say was hard.

"It's okay, you can tell me," he said, forgetting all about his decision that it wasn't a good idea to get emotionally involved.

For a long moment, she seemed to be consider-ing whether she wanted to continue. "When I was twenty, I had a baby…a little girl. This year, she will turn nineteen. I—I gave her up for adoption." As he watched, her face crumpled and she put her head down, her shoulders shaking with sobs.

Dan got up, walked around the table, and pulled her up and into his arms. Holding her trembling body, he knew that his feelings for her had already passed the point of friendship and morphed into something a hundred times stronger, something that might be his undoing if he wasn't careful.

When her tears eased, she seemed to realize

where she was, and she stiffened. Immediately, he loosened his hold.

"I—I'm sorry," she said. She dug into the pocket of her jeans for a tissue and blew her nose.

"Nothing to be sorry for."

"I always seem to be crying on your shoulder."

Trying to lighten the atmosphere, he smiled. "That's what shoulders are for." Seeing that his attempt to make her feel better hadn't worked, he said quietly, "Do you want to tell me about it?"

She took a long, shaky breath. "Sure you want to hear?"

"Yes, I do."

"How about if I warm up our coffee first?"

"Okay."

"Want another piece of pie?"

"What the hell." He grinned. "You only live once."

Her smile was shaky, but at least it was a smile.

A few minutes later, second cups of coffee in front of them along with Dan's second piece of pie, she began to talk again.

"Gregg's and my parents died when we were sixteen. It was very hard on us, especially me."

Dan thought of his own parents, in their seventies and still healthy and strong and living on their own. He knew he was lucky. "That's tough. How did they die?"

"It was an accident. They were driving back from a wedding in Pittsburgh. Gregg and I didn't go because there was a big basketball tournament that weekend, and Ivy had a chance to go to state. Gregg played on the team, he was first string." She smiled nostalgically. "I was a cheerleader."

He smiled, too. "I can see you as cheerleader."

Her smile faded. "They were on the interstate. The weather was bad. It was snowing really hard. There was a travel advisory. They shouldn't have been on the road, but they were anxious to get home because Gregg's and my birthday was the following day. Anyway, the driver of one of those big tour buses that bands use lost control of it and jumped the median. My parents' car was hit head-on, and they were killed instantly. Four other people in two other cars died, too. It was awful."

"Geez, Glynnis, that's horrible. I'm really sorry."

"Thank you. I took it hard, harder than Gregg. He's always been tougher than me." She picked up her mug and drank some of her coffee. In the silence, the ticking of the kitchen clock seemed loud. "I was really close to my dad. Sometimes I think that's why, in the years since, I gravitated toward older men." Her mouth twisted. "You know. That old cliché. Looking for a father figure."

"So what happened after the accident? Did you and Gregg live on your own?"

"No. Our Aunt Rita—actually, my mother's aunt—came to live with us until we graduated from high school." Her face softened at the mention of her great-aunt. "She was a sweetheart. Even though I was heartbroken over my parents' death, I loved Aunt Rita. It helped to have her."

"Where is she now?"

"She passed away seven years ago. She was eighty-one years old. I still miss her. Anyway, after high school, Gregg and I both went to Ohio State. He wanted to go to Duke because of their basketball program, but he didn't want to leave me." She lifted her coffee cup again, but she didn't drink any, just held it in her hands as if she were warming them. "He acted like it was no big deal, but I knew better. He'd gotten an athletic scholarship to Duke. It was a lot to give up."

It *was* a lot to give up. Dan thought about his brothers and sisters. He loved them all, but he couldn't imagine being as selfless as Gregg had been with Glynnis. Of course, Dan was one of seven. And his parents were alive. Plus, he'd always heard that twins had a different relationship than other siblings had.

"At the end of my freshman year," she continued, "I fell in love with one of my professors. I knew he was married, but he told me he was separated from his wife and they were getting a divorce." She finally put her cup down. "What can I say? I was young. Stupid. Naive. And needy." She looked away, shook her head. "It sounds really dumb now. But I honestly thought he loved me. I thought we were soul mates. I thought we were going to be married."

What she was telling him was an old story and had happened to thousands of silly young girls—but somehow Glynnis had seemed smarter than that.

Sure, she'd been married to a man who turned out to be someone other than what he'd pretended to be, but that was *his* shortcoming, not hers, despite what she'd said earlier.

"You're shocked, aren't you?"

"No, of course not. Like you said, you were young. When we're young we do a lot of dumb things." He told himself he had no right to feel disappointed in her. Hell, he'd made a really dumb choice himself, and he'd been older than her.

"It's okay, whatever you're thinking. I understand. Believe me, I understand. I hate what I did. I hate that I was taken in by Philip. That was his name. Philip Van Horne. Sounds like something out of a gothic novel, doesn't it?" She shook her head. "Long story even longer." Her voice was flat now. Tired. "He and his wife reconciled. He told me we could still see each other, though. Just as if it were no big deal. I'll never forget that day. Realizing that he never loved me. That all I was to him was a willing body, some easy sex with a silly, adoring student."

"Glynnis…"

"Gregg and I had made arrangements to meet after my classes that day. Have a Coke or something together. He took one look at my face and knew something was wrong. I told him everything." Now the emotion was back in her voice. "It was awful. He went crazy. He stormed over to Philip's house. He…" She shuddered. "He beat Philip up pretty bad.

I was so afraid Philip might press charges against him, but he didn't."

Dan's hands had fisted. He would have liked nothing better than to put those hands around that scumball Van Horne's neck. He didn't blame Gregg in the least for his reaction. If it had been one of his sisters, he'd have done the same thing. Only he might have killed the bastard.

"I dropped out of school. Went to L.A. where my godmother lives. I needed to lick my wounds for a while. Three weeks later, I discovered I was pregnant. I didn't know what to do. I agonized for days. Finally I came to the conclusion that I couldn't keep the baby. I had no husband. And no marketable skills. In fact, I'd never held a job. There was no way I could make more than a minimal living, and even though our parents had left us some money, it wouldn't have lasted long if I'd had to support myself and a child.

"If I'd had any kind of support system, I might have been brave enough to try keeping the baby. Don't get me wrong, Gregg is wonderful. He would have done anything to help me out, but I couldn't expect him to take on that kind of responsibility. He still had more than two years of college. I couldn't take that away from him. I decided if I wanted the baby to have the kind of start in life Gregg and I had had, I really had no choice but to give the baby up for adoption. I wasn't even going to say anything to Gregg, but I hated having that kind of secret between us. Somehow, telling him made things easier for me. Probably because he told me he thought I was doing the right thing."

"I think you did the right thing, too."

She nodded thoughtfully. "My head knows it was a good decision." Her eyes met his again. "But the heart is a different matter entirely."

Dan could certainly understand that. In the last days of Mona's life, when she'd been suffering so terribly, he'd known that death would release her from her pain, but he hadn't wanted her to die, because he couldn't bear the thought of a world without her in it. "Did you live with your godmother during your pregnancy?"

"Yes. Aunt Sarah—she's not really my aunt, but I always called her that—was so good to me. At the time, her husband was alive, and he was wonderful, too. They said I could stay as long as I needed to. I stayed until it was time to have the baby. She was born at one of those private clinics—the kind where they work with an adoption agency and take care of everything for you."

"Do you know who adopted your daughter?"

She shook her head. "No." She folded and re-folded her napkin. "I've thought about it so much, though. On every one of her birthdays I've imagined where she might be, what she might look like, what she might be doing, if she ever thinks about me." She swallowed. "I think about what might have been. I think about how if I'd only been stronger or braver…" She looked away, but not before he saw the sheen of tears.

He could have told her he'd done the same. On Mona's birthdays, he always thought about what might have been. But this wasn't about him, so he kept quiet. Glynnis needed to talk, and the best thing he could do was listen.

"I think if I just knew she was happy, I'd be all right. It's horrible to second-guess yourself. Wonder if you did the right thing, after all." She looked away. "Sometimes I feel so guilty."

"Have you thought about trying to find her?"

She nodded. "But something always stops me. I'm not sure—"

"Not sure what?"

"She…she might not want to know me."

"You'll never know if you don't try."

"It's just that I've made so many mistakes in my life. I wouldn't want to make another."

He nodded. He understood that, too. "I could do some research for you. I've got lots of connections."

"What kind of research?"

"Well, I know there's some kind of international registry where kids who've been adopted can register and say if they're interested in meeting their birth parents and vice versa. I could check it out for you. Then, if you want to, you could register and then if some day your daughter was interested in contacting you, she'd have a way to do that."

Glynnis bit her bottom lip.

"Glynnis?" he said gently.

"But…but what if I find out something I'd rather not know?"

Dan thought about all the times he'd nearly called Angelina Flores to see how she and her family were doing and to beg for her forgiveness. And how many times he'd been too chicken and so he continued to hide here in Ivy and pretend the deaths of her sister and nephew hadn't happened. "We can only escape from our past for so long," he said reflectively. "Sooner or later, to move on, we have to confront it."

"Are…are you talking about Mona?"

Hearing his daughter's name on her lips gave him a jolt, and for the space of about ten seconds, he was furious with Kat—because she had to be the one to have told Glynnis about Mona. But the fury died quickly. Of course she'd told Glynnis. He wouldn't have expected anything less from his sister. And truthfully, he was glad Glynnis knew. "No. I have no regrets when it comes to Mona. I did everything in my power to make her life a happy one, and I think I succeeded. I'm talking about something else."

"Do…do you want to talk about it?"

He shook his head. "Not yet. I just want to say that we all make mistakes we have to live with. You're not alone."

She nodded agreement, but her eyes were bleak.

He wished he could offer something more, but could think of nothing that would help. Maybe the best thing he could do was go home and give her some time alone. He finished off his coffee and stood. "It's getting late. And I can see you're tired."

She didn't deny it.

He picked up his dish and cup.

"Just leave those."

"My mother would disown me if I did." It was a feeble attempt to lighten the atmosphere, and he knew it. He placed the dirty dishes in the sink.

She walked him to the front door. Before opening it, she put her hand on his arm and said, "Dan, thanks for listening tonight. I—I hope you don't think less of me now."

He covered her hand with his. "C'mon, Glynnis. I told you. Nobody's perfect. Hell, if you *were* perfect, you'd scare me."

Her smile was tremulous. She started to say something else, but the words died on her lips. Suddenly, all time seemed suspended as their gazes held.

Afterwards, Dan would never know who moved first. He only knew that a moment later, she was in his arms, and he was kissing her—first gently, then, as the kiss went on, with more and more urgency. God, she felt good. She fitted into his arms as if she'd been made for him, her soft lips yielding to his, her mouth opening in sweet welcome as he probed with his tongue.

His head swam as the kiss went on and on.

Finally, he reluctantly released her. For a long moment, they simply stared at each other, each too shaken to speak. Then in a ragged voice he hardly recognized as his, he muttered, "Good night. I'll call you tomorrow."

Not waiting for her answer, he opened the door and walked out.

Glynnis trembled with desire as Dan slowly undressed her. First her sweater, then her slacks, joined her shoes and socks on the floor of the bedroom. He smiled when he saw her lacy yellow underwear.

"Nice," he whispered, trailing kisses over her breasts and then down her belly and slowly back up.

Glynnis moaned as his mouth found her nipple through her bra. She clutched at him, pressing him closer. When he raised his head, she whispered, "Don't stop."

In answer, he unclasped her bra. When the cold air hit her uncovered breasts, she shivered.

"Are you cold?"

"No," she lied.

"You won't be cold for long, I promise." He began to tug her panties down. "What's this?" he said, running his finger across the small scar on her belly.

"Cesarean section when I had Livvy," she managed, even though his hand had moved lower and was now delving in a place and way that made her gasp and arch into his touch.

He bent his head, and while his hand continued to work its magic, he kissed the scar, then moved his lips lower and lower still.

Glynnis bit back a scream as the first wave of

*pleasure seized her. But when Dan gripped her hips
and pushed his tongue deeper, she couldn't help herself.*

Glynnis sat up so abruptly, she banged her head
on the headboard. Her heart was pounding wildly,
and for a moment, she was disoriented.

Dan. Where was he?

She looked around, and slowly, reality came back.
Dan wasn't there. They hadn't been making love.
She'd been dreaming. Disappointment poured
through her. Disappointment and an aching sense of
loss.

Had she screamed out loud?

Quickly, she got out of bed and tiptoed down the
hall. In turn, she checked Michael's and Olivia's
rooms. Both were sleeping soundly.

Relieved, but still shaky, she went back to her
bedroom and put on her robe and slippers. The digital clock at her bedside read 3:12.

Walking out to the living room, she stood at the
bay window and looked out at the silent street. Snow
glistened under the street lamp at the corner. Nothing in her range of vision moved.

She hugged herself.

Dan.

The memory of his kiss and the way it had made
her feel was all she could think of.

The kiss had changed everything between them.

And yet it changed nothing.

She was still a mess, still in no shape to begin a

romantic relationship. Certainly in no shape to begin a sexual relationship.

But, oh, she wanted him.

Obviously, she thought wryly. Her body had still not calmed from her erotic dream. It still yearned for something she couldn't have, for if there was one thing Glynnis knew for sure in a world where she wasn't certain of much, it was this: she was not going to become sexually involved with anyone unless she was absolutely sure it would lead to something permanent.

Because this time she had more than just her own needs to consider. This time she had two children. Children who could not handle the loss of another man in their lives.

Chapter Nine

Dan had a bad night.

To begin with, he had a hard time falling asleep. He couldn't stop thinking about everything that had happened between him and Glynnis that night—especially that kiss!—and then once he finally did fall asleep, he had disturbing dreams, one of which was a reenactment of the night that had haunted him since he left Chicago.

He kept seeing that apartment. The gunshots fired through the door. The fellow cop who had fallen with a mortal wound. He and Jack and the other officers firing back. Jack kicking in the door. Three of them storming into the apartment and discovering that the drug dealer hadn't been alone. That his girlfriend and her little boy had been there with him.

He relived the horror and the feelings of despair

when he looked at that child. Mixed up in the dream was Mona and then Glynnis and Glynnis's baby. The dream segued from the real to the imagined—an exhausting, mixed-up jumble.

Dan woke up with a pounding headache. He wasn't sure if he was glad he didn't have to go into work or not. At least work might have taken his mind off the things that troubled him, especially Glynnis and their relationship.

He couldn't stop thinking about that kiss. Why had he kissed her? He'd known better, yet he'd kissed her anyway. Now their relationship would change. Because even if they both wanted to, there was no way they could pretend the kiss hadn't happened.

Dammit, anyway.

He was an idiot. He'd told himself one thing, then done another.

He'd never found himself in this kind of situation before. Not that he'd dated that many women since his divorce, but in the last few years, he'd had a couple of short-lived relationships, and they'd all followed a predictable pattern. Either he or the woman or both of them would quickly decide they weren't interested enough to take the relationship from casual dates to the next level, or they took it to the next level and enjoyed the sex as long as it lasted. Then they parted company amicably.

Neither scenario applied to Glynnis.

First of all, he *was* interested and from her reaction to that kiss, she was, too. However, she was not the type of woman who would go to the next level casually. Even if she had been, there were the children to consider.

So if he and Glynnis were to become sexually intimate, it would mean they were committing to each other. And as much as Dan thought that might be a possibility for the future, he wasn't ready to take that kind of step yet, and he was doubly sure after what she'd told him last night that Glynnis wasn't, either.

So where did that leave them? He'd already figured out he couldn't pretend the kiss hadn't happened. So should he talk to Glynnis frankly? Say something like, *I really like you a lot but I think we need to cool it?* What if saying something like that hurt her feelings and completely ruined their relationship?

He wished he could talk to somebody, get some advice. Not Kat, though. He already knew what she'd say. He thought about his brothers. Two of them lived in the Ivy area. But even though he had a good relationship with both, they'd never confided in each other about personal stuff.

And Dan had never had a lot of friends. Cops rarely did. Usually their friends were other cops, because the nature of the job didn't leave them time or energy for developing outside friendships, but mainly because civilians didn't understand cops. It was too hard finding any kind of common meeting ground.

The closest friend Dan had ever had was Jack

Perry, his old partner from the Chicago PD. The two hadn't talked much since Dan left the Chicago force, but that wasn't Jack's fault. He'd called Dan half a dozen times. It was Dan who hadn't been receptive. They *had* exchanged a couple of e-mails, but that was the extent of their contact. The trouble was, Jack was associated with all the dark stuff Dan didn't want to think about.

But it's time, Dan thought. *I need to practice what I preach. Face the past so I can move on, just like I told Glynnis she should.*

So after showering and shaving and having his breakfast, Dan picked up his cell phone and punched in the familiar numbers.

"Hey, Danny boy! It's been a long time. How's it goin' out there in the boonies?" Jack sounded exactly the same.

It was a relief to know Jack wasn't mad at him. "Ivy's not the boonies."

"So you say. Maybe if I'd get an invite to visit, I could check it out for myself."

Now Dan smiled. "Tell you what. Why don't you plan to bring Annette down some weekend in the next month or so? I'll e-mail you tomorrow and let you know when I'm off, see if we can find a good time."

"Afraid it'll have to be just me, buddy. Annette and I, we're history."

"What?" Jack and Annette Rice, an assistant Cook County D.A., had been joined at the hip for at least three years now. "What happened?"

"She met somebody else. Gave me the old heave-ho."

"Geez, Jack, I'm sorry."

There was an audible sigh from the other end of the phone. "Yeah, me, too. But I've got nobody but myself to blame. I knew she wanted to get married— I mean, she made no secret of it—and I was dragging my feet."

"How come? I thought you were nuts about her."

"I was, but you know…I already had one bad marriage behind me. I wasn't sure I wanted to take another chance. We cops don't have a great track record when it comes to building good relationships."

"Yeah, I know, but hell, Annette. She seemed perfect for you. I don't think you'll ever find anyone better."

"Are you tryin' to make me feel bad?"

This was said in a lighthearted way, but Dan heard an undercurrent that made him hurt for Jack. "No, I'm just sorry 'cause I liked Annette."

"How about you? Things goin' okay?"

"Yeah, they're goin' pretty good."

"You like it there?"

"It's not real exciting, but that's what I wanted."

"You still beatin' yourself up over that Flores thing?"

"I'm trying not to."

"The sister sued the city, you know."

"Did she?"

"Yeah. I heard the legal eagles settled out of court. Guess they figured this was one case they couldn't beat."

"I'm glad. I hope she got a lot of money and I hope it helps."

"Listen, Danny, what happened, that wasn't your fault. That dealer was shooting at us. We only shot back in self-defense. No one knew that kid was in the apartment."

For a long moment, Dan didn't answer. When he did, his voice was strained. "Two people died that night, Jack."

"Yeah, I know, but it's the kid dying that's been eating at you."

It would do no good to deny the truth of that statement. Jack knew Dan too well.

"Anyway, it was his mother's fault more than anyone's. What the hell was she doin' with that slime bucket, anyway? You gotta let it go, man. I have."

"I know." Logically, Dan did know. Internal Affairs had made a thorough investigation. Dan, Jack and the two other cops with them had been cleared of any wrongdoing. In fact, Jack and Dan had received commendations for busting a prominent drug ring. The fact that Dan had refused to accept his was incidental. "Let's change the subject, okay?"

"Okay. So…you met any good-lookin' babes yet?"

"Maybe."

"No kiddin'? Who is she?"

"Somebody I met on a case."

"What kind of case?"

So Dan told him about Olivia's abduction.

"Is it serious?" Jack said when Dan had finished.

"I don't know. We just started seeing each other." Suddenly Dan didn't want to discuss Glynnis anymore. He'd been wrong to think he needed to talk about his feelings. What he needed was some time to sort them out on his own.

"Well, I'm looking forward to meeting this chick," Jack said. "If you're still seeing her when I come."

They talked a while more and then signed off, with Dan once more promising to e-mail Jack his schedule.

Dan had no sooner hung up than his cell phone rang. He recognized his sister Renny's number.

"Hey, Dan, glad I caught you. You at work or home?"

"I'm off today, so I'm home."

"Good, because I wanted to discuss Mom and Dad's anniversary."

"When is it?"

Renny laughed. "Geez, you guys are unbelievable. Why is it always up to me and Kat and Shawn to remember all the important family stuff?"

"'Cause guys are missing that important-date-recall gene, that's why. Remembering dates is woman's work."

"If you were here, I'd deck you for that sexist comment."

"Sexist? That wasn't sexist. It's a known fact. Women are programmed different than we are."

She laughed. "You're hopeless. Anyway, write this down somewhere. Where you won't lose it. On February 14th—that's Valentine's Day, in case you can't remember that either—Mom and Dad will celebrate their fiftieth anniversary. Shawn and Kat and I have talked and we think we need to throw them a big party."

"That sounds good."

"I'm glad you agree, because a party won't be cheap and everyone needs to kick in...and help, too."

"I'll do anything you need. Just point me in the right direction."

"Good. We have several ideas about where to have it. The K of C Hall, for one, but if we do that, we'll have to have it catered. Or the AOH Hall, but it's not as nice as the K of C. We also thought about Costello's. They've got a beautiful private room, but their food is pricey. You have any ideas?"

"Me? I don't know enough about what's around here anymore." Then Dan had a thought. "What about Antonclli's?"

"We actually considered Antonelli's, but their private room isn't big enough. Mom and Dad have lived here all of their lives. With all the family and all their friends, we could end up with more than a hundred people. But we could use Antonelli's to cater the party if they can handle one that big. They've got some of the best food in town."

She was obviously thinking out loud.

"Anyway," she continued, "we're gonna meet at my place tonight to talk about all this. Can you come?"

"Sure. What time?"

"Six. I thought I'd order some pizza. That okay with you?"

"It's great. I'll bring the beer."

For some reason, talking to Jack and Renny had helped clear Dan's head. After saying goodbye to his sister, he realized what he needed to do, at least as far as the situation with Glynnis was concerned.

And he wasn't going to take the coward's way out and do it over the phone.

"Want to come and have dinner with us this afternoon? I'm roasting a pork tenderloin."

The invitation came from Sabrina. She, Gregg, Glynnis and the children were standing outside St. Catherine's after attending the nine-thirty service.

"Thanks, but I have tests to grade and bills to pay and really need the afternoon at home," Glynnis said.

The truth was, she was afraid her emotions were still in too much turmoil to spend hours in the company of her brother and sister-in-law, both of whom were much too astute when it came to Glynnis and her moods.

She was still upset that she hadn't been able to control herself the night before. Plus, she needed to figure out what she was going to say to Dan when he called.

"Mom, I want to go," Michael said.

"I'm sorry, Michael. I just have too much to do today."

"But Mom..."

"Michael, please don't whine." Her tone was sharper than she'd meant it to be. Seeing the hurt look on Michael's face, she immediately felt bad. And guilty. "I'm sorry, honey. I—"

"How about letting the kids come home with us?" Gregg interrupted.

"That's a great idea," Sabrina said. "You can go home, get your work done, then join us later. I won't have dinner ready until two at the earliest."

Glynnis couldn't think of another excuse. Besides, three hours alone sounded wonderful. She could get her papers graded and checks written and also figure out exactly what she needed to say to Dan when they talked. "Well, if you're sure..."

"Okay, it's settled," Gregg said. "C'mon, kids, let's find the car."

Glynnis kissed the children goodbye after warning them to behave, then climbed into her own car and headed home. The message light was blinking on her phone when she walked in the door. She pressed the Play button.

"Glynnis, hi. It's Dan. I wanted to come by and talk to you for a few minutes. Give me a call when you get home, okay?" Then he left her his number, saying it was his cell phone.

Glynnis's heart began to beat faster. What did he

want to talk about? That kiss? Oh, God. She wasn't ready. And yet, maybe she was. Because no matter how she cut it, she knew there was no way she could keep seeing Dan unless they agreed that from now on, they would have to see each other as friends only. Right now, anything more was impossible.

Taking a deep breath, she picked up the phone.

Thirty minutes later, Glynnis's doorbell rang. Composing herself, she walked to the door. But when she opened the door and saw Dan, looking far too handsome in his dark overcoat and the cashmere scarf she'd given him for Christmas, she found it hard to keep breathing normally.

"Hi," he said.

"Hi." She willed herself to give him a casual smile. Her wayward heart was beating too fast as she stepped aside so he could come in.

He took off his coat and scarf, hanging both on the clothes tree in the corner of the foyer. Underneath he wore a bright blue sweater, jeans and black boots.

"Do you want to sit in the living room or the kitchen? I've got fresh coffee." She made a conscious effort not to look at his mouth, but her gaze seemed rooted to the spot.

"The kitchen's fine."

Was he feeling as awkward as she was? she wondered as she led the way.

Some of her awkwardness was dispelled by the

simple act of setting out coffee mugs, cream and sugar, then pouring a mugful for each of them. "Are you hungry? I've got some cinnamon coffee cake."

He shook his head. "I had a late breakfast, thanks."

Glynnis couldn't think of anything else to stall whatever was coming, so she sat down. Avoiding his gaze, she put cream in her coffee and added sweetener.

"Glynnis…"

No longer able to put off the moment of reckoning, she lifted her gaze to meet his.

"About last night…" he began.

His eyes were so blue.

"I just wanted to apologize for taking—"

"There's no need to apologize," she hurriedly interjected.

"I think there is. I took advantage of the—"

"No, you didn't." She rushed on, knowing if she didn't get this out in a hurry, she wouldn't be able to say it. "You didn't take advantage of anything. We were both kind of emotional, that's all. Look, I don't want you to feel awkward about it. It was just something that happened." She took a deep breath. It was time for honesty. "The truth is, I'm very attracted to you, and I wanted you to kiss me, but I think we both know I'm not ready for any kind of…of intimate relationship. Not yet. It's too soon and I'm too…" She laughed self-consciously. "Too screwed up."

"C'mon, Glynnis, you're not screwed up. I agree

that you've got some stuff to work out, but hell, so do I. So do most people."

"Thanks, but it's the same thing, isn't it?" Her smile was wry. "What I'm trying to say, and not very well, is that I hope we can still be friends, but I'm not ready for anything more right now."

He smiled. "That's exactly what I thought. Think," he corrected.

She could hear the relief in his voice. Part of her was glad he agreed with what she'd said. The other part of her felt a sharp pang of loss, because what if friendship was all she'd ever have now? What if she'd completely killed all chance of anything else?

Dan had just walked into the station when the phone on his desk rang. Slinging his jacket onto a nearby chair, he grabbed the phone. "Lieutenant O'Neill."

"Dan?" It was his mother.

"Hi, Ma."

"Dan, listen, I've been trying to call you on your cell phone for the last twenty minutes and I kept getting your voice mail."

"Yeah, sorry. The battery conked out on me 'cause I forgot to charge it last night."

"Dan, are you sitting down?"

Dan's heart thumped in alarm. Had something happened to his dad?

"You're not going to believe this." She took an audible breath. "Cindy called here."

Dan's mouth dropped open. "Cindy? My ex-wife, Cindy?"

"Yes."

"What the hell does *she* want?" Jesus. He hadn't heard a word from Cindy since she'd walked out on him and Mona thirteen years ago. Not one stinking word. It was like she'd dropped off the face of the earth. He hadn't known if she was living or dead. And it wasn't just him she'd ignored. She hadn't even written to Mona. Not a birthday card. Not a Christmas card. Nothing.

"I don't know, son," his mother was saying. "She called and wanted to know where she could find you. I guess she tried the Chicago PD and someone there told her you'd moved back to Ivy."

"So did you tell her where I was?"

"Well, I did tell her how to reach you. I thought…" She stopped. "Did I do the wrong thing?"

He sighed. Now that the shock had worn off, he was almost glad Cindy had reappeared. He had a thing or two to say to her. Then maybe he really *would* be able to put the past behind him, on that score, anyway. "No, it's okay."

"I just wanted to warn you that she might show up at the station. I gave her your cell phone number, but I didn't want to tell her where you lived in case you really didn't want to see her. But she's not stupid, Dan. She'll figure out that you're probably working for the Ivy police, since being a cop is the only thing you've ever done."

"Yeah, you're probably right. Okay, thanks, Ma. I'll let you know what happens."

"Okay. And Dan?"

"Yeah?"

"If she *does* show up…"

"What?"

"Never mind. It's none of my business."

"Hey, you're my mother. You can say what you think."

"Well, it's just that hate is a negative emotion, you know?"

"Yeah, I know."

"What's done is done," she added softly.

"I know. Don't worry. I won't kill her."

She laughed uneasily, and they said goodbye.

Dan quietly put the phone back in its cradle. He was sitting on a corner of his desk, and for a long moment, he didn't move. Cindy. He could see her in his mind just as plain as if she were standing in front of him.

His marriage to Cindy had been a disaster from day one. But that didn't change the fact that he'd been hot for her from the first moment he'd seen her. She'd been hired as a cocktail waitress at a local pub that he and his buddies frequented a couple of times a week. She'd waited on them that first night, and he couldn't take his eyes off her.

She'd had an eye-popping body. A *Baywatch* babe kind of body, curvy and sexy. She'd been tanned, too, whereas the rest of them all had Chicago winter-white skin. Her tan probably came from a tanning bed, but who cared? And topping it all off, she'd had masses of blond hair that hung halfway down her back. In her cocktail waitress uniform of tight black miniskirt and figure-hugging white sweater, she'd been something to see.

She'd zeroed in on him right away, giving him sultry looks and smiles that promised all kinds of delights. He'd waited until her shift was over at two, even though he was on duty at eight. They'd gone to her apartment, hardly in the door before they'd begun tearing at each other's clothes.

The sex had been fantastic, the best he'd ever had—not that he was all that experienced. Hell, he was only twenty-two. Even so, he'd heard the guys talking. This girl was one hot tamale, practically insatiable. Somehow Dan had crawled into work the next day, but he'd spent the day thinking about her; every time he did, his body reacted. He could hardly wait to see her again.

From then on, they'd spent every spare minute together, and most of those minutes were spent in her bed. He couldn't get enough of her. Part of him knew they were very different. Hell, Cindy had barely made it out of high school. She'd admitted she hated school. She never cracked a book, didn't read the newspaper, had no idea what was going on in the world.

The only things she cared about were clothes, makeup, sex and her fantasy of making it as a big-time model.

Looking back, Dan could see just how blind he'd been. But at the time, his hormones were raging, and all he could think about was how much he wanted her.

Four months after they met, they were married. His family was appalled—he'd known that—although no one but his sister Kat—more sensible and world-wise than he'd been at seventeen—had had the guts to say so.

"Geez, Dan, I thought you had more sense," she'd said, rolling her eyes.

He'd bristled. "What's that supposed to mean?"

"You know what it means."

He'd glared at her. "Humor me. Spell it out."

"Okay, in plain English…you're not exactly thinking with your brain. I mean it's obvious that all the two of you have going for you is sex. When the thrill of that wears off, what's going to be left? I predict you'll be bored with her in a year. And Cindy might not even last *that* long."

He sighed. Kat had been right. It hadn't even taken him a year to realize what a big mistake he'd made. They'd managed to stay together four years, just long enough for Cindy to give birth to their daughter Mona and to decide she'd had enough when Mona was two weeks shy of her second birthday.

One night, exhausted from a week-long stakeout that had finally wrapped up, Dan came home from work to find Mona in the care of their next-door neighbor and Cindy gone. She hadn't even left a note. She'd just packed up all her belongings, cleaned out their savings account of most of what was in it and disappeared.

He'd heard nothing from her or about her since then. And truth be told, he hadn't missed her. But Mona had. She'd cried every night for a week after Cindy left. She'd started sucking her thumb—which she'd never done before—and began waking up several times a night. It was obvious she was having nightmares, although she'd been too young to articulate them. She'd just cried and clung to him and refused to go back to bed in her crib. Finally, he'd had no choice but to let her sleep with him in his bed. It took three months before she could sleep through the night and another three before she'd sleep alone.

He'd hated Cindy in those dark days. Thought if he'd had her there, he'd strangle her.

But gradually Mona had forgotten her mother. She and Dan bonded in a way he knew he'd never have had if it hadn't been for the fact he was raising her alone.

Even though it was tough to be a single father, especially one with a job like his, it had been a good life. He'd divorced Cindy and devoted himself to his daughter and his career, in that order. He'd even begun dating again when the unthinkable happened. A month after Mona's fifth birthday, she was diagnosed with inoperable brain cancer. Seven months and multiple chemotherapy and radiation treatments later, she died.

Dan was devastated, and even though that had been more than nine years ago, the memory of those terrible days could still cut as deeply as they had in the beginning. Each time he looked at a picture of Mona or remembered something she'd done or said, or saw a little girl her age, he was reminded again of what he'd lost. Lately, those memories had been coming more often.

"Hey, Dan, you still alive over there?"

"Huh?" Dan had been so deeply lost in his memories, he had forgotten where he was. Now he looked at Elena, who gestured to the waiting area on the other side of her desk.

"You've got a visitor," she mouthed, her dark eyes big and curious.

Dan braced himself for what he knew would be one hell of a reunion.

Chapter Ten

Sure enough, Cindy sat on one of the wooden benches in the waiting area. She was now in her late thirties, but she still looked good. The years had been kind to her, although as Dan came closer, he saw some fine lines around her eyes and mouth that her skillful makeup didn't quite hide. She'd learned something about how to dress, though. Her dark blue pants and matching sweater, although fitted and flattering, could have been safely worn to a PTA meeting. Folded on the bench beside her was a camel hair coat, leather gloves, and a thick beige scarf.

"Hello, Dan." She stood, her blue eyes meeting his unflinchingly. "Surprised?"

Something about her arrogance—or was it just plain stupidity?—ignited the flame of fury he'd felt in those early days when Mona was so heartbroken by her mother's desertion.

But he kept his voice even when he answered. "Considering I didn't know if you were alive or dead, I guess you could say that, yeah, I'm surprised."

She shrugged. "I didn't really see the point in keeping in touch. I knew you were probably glad to see the back of me, so why bother?"

"Why bother? Why *bother?*" He stared at her. What a bitch she was. Why hadn't he seen it? "You just forgot you had a child?"

She flinched. "No, I didn't forget. But I…I thought she was better off without me. I wasn't a very good mother."

"No, you weren't," he said coldly.

"I'm sorry, Dan. I know it was wrong of me to leave like that, and I *should* have kept in touch, but I was ashamed."

He snorted.

"I *was*. You don't have to believe me, but I *was*."

"Okay, fine. You were. I don't want to discuss it. All I want to know is, why the hell are you here now?"

She gave him a wary look. "I—I want to see Mona."

He felt as if she'd punched him. "You want to see Mona," he repeated flatly.

She raised her chin. "Yes."

His mouth twisted. "Well, *sweetheart,* you're out of luck."

Her eyes narrowed. "You know, Dan, I didn't have

to come here and ask your permission. I could've just found out where she's going to school and gone to see her without telling you. After all, I'm her mother."

"Some mother."

"Look, I already said I'm sorry. I can't change what I did, but I have some rights here."

"Oh, yeah?"

"Yeah."

He almost smiled. If the situation hadn't been so damned terrible, if it didn't hurt so much, he would have. Suddenly he wanted to hurt her the way she'd hurt their daughter. He wanted to pay her back for all those nights Mona had cried. For all those times she'd sadly told a playmate that she didn't have a mommy. For all those birthdays and Christmases that Cindy had ignored.

"Rights or not," he said, "you're out of luck. You're about nine years too late."

"Fine," she bit off. "Be that way. But I'm going to see her, with or without your permission."

Now he did smile, and anyone observing would have shivered at its coldness. "Hope you like digging."

She frowned. "What does that mean?"

"Just what I said. Hope you like digging. You see, Cindy, your daughter, the one you abandoned so easily, the one that cried for you every night after you left, that beautiful child who deserved so much better than she got, is now six feet under. She died nine years ago—" Suddenly he couldn't talk. Tears clogged his throat. Fighting them, he managed to finish. "Right before her sixth birthday, of a brain tumor. She's buried in my family's plot at Calvary Cemetery here in Ivy."

She stared at him, shock leaching the color from her face. "No," she whispered.

"Yes."

She shook her head, eyes stricken. She reached for the back of the bench, obviously in need of support.

Suddenly all his anger evaporated, and he was ashamed of himself. "Look, I'm sorry. I shouldn't have dumped it on you like that."

She bowed her head.

Dammit. He felt like a real jerk. No matter what she'd done or not done, she hadn't deserved this. "Hey." His voice was gentle. "You want a Coke? Or some coffee?"

She took a long, shuddering breath. "Sure."

"Put your coat on. There's a coffee shop right across the street. I'll get my coat and be right back."

"Elena," he said as he walked back into the bullpen. "I'm gonna take a break. Be back in about thirty minutes." He could see interest in the dispatcher's wide brown eyes. She'd probably heard every word he and Cindy had exchanged.

"Okay, I'll beep you if I need you."

Ten minutes later, he and Cindy were seated across from each other in a red leather booth, steaming cups of coffee in front of them.

"I really am sorry," he said again. "I was a jerk back there."

She shook her head. "I don't blame you. I deserved that."

"No, you didn't."

"Let's not argue about it, okay?"

"Sure." He drank some of his coffee and waited.

"Would you tell me about her?"

"What do you want to know?"

"Did…" She wet her lips. "Did she really cry every night?"

"At first. But little kids forget fast. The crying only lasted a couple of weeks." There was no sense telling her about the nightmares.

"Was she sick for a long time?"

"Seven months from the time she was diagnosed."

She swallowed. "Did…did she suffer?"

He remembered how, near the end, they'd kept her doped up with pain killers. But there was no point in telling her that, either. "Some. Mostly from the chemo. It made her really sick." He attempted a smile. "She was a little trouper, though."

"I should have been there."

What did she want him to say? What *could* he say? *Yes, you should have.* What purpose would heaping guilt on her serve? It sure wouldn't bring Mona back.

She swiped at her eyes. Looked out the window. Sighed. Then turned her gaze back to him. "You get married again?"

Dan shook his head.

"Me, neither."

"Where are you living now?" he asked.

"In L.A."

He wanted to ask what she did to earn a living, but before he could, she volunteered the information.

"I'm modeling, you know."

"No, I didn't know that."

"I mostly do catalog work. Lingerie. I'm in real demand." She smiled proudly, sitting up straighter and preening a bit.

Yes, he could see how she'd be perfect for that kind of work. No one looked at your face when you modeled lingerie, and her body still looked as good as it had fifteen years ago. In fact, it might even look better. He wondered if she'd had a boob job.

"When did you leave Chicago?" she asked.

"About six months ago."

"Oh. Do…you *like* it here?"

The way she'd phrased the question, putting the emphasis on *like* told Dan she couldn't imagine anyone wanting to actually live here.

He nodded. "Yeah. I like it a lot."

"I never thought you were the small-town type."

"We never knew each other very well, did we?"

Her eyes met his. "No, I guess not."

She didn't seem to know anything else to say after that, and neither did Dan. By now, they'd finished their coffee and their waitress came by to see if they wanted a refill. Both Dan and Cindy shook their heads no. Dan paid the bill, and they walked outside into the cold January afternoon.

"So where are you off to now? Back to L.A.?" he asked.

"Not right away. I have a job in Miami first."

He nodded. Suddenly he felt damned awkward. How did you say goodbye to your ex-wife whom up until an hour ago, you'd hated?

"Um, Dan? Would you…I mean…I don't suppose you could take me to see Mona's grave?"

The question took him unaware, and for just a second, he wanted to tell her she'd forfeited all right to see Mona's grave. But as soon as the thought formed, he was ashamed of it. Yet he wasn't sure he could handle going to the cemetery with her. But how could he refuse? "Sure, I'll take you."

After calling Elena to tell her he'd be gone longer than he'd thought, he led Cindy to his car. They were silent on the short ride to the cemetery.

Dan drove through the main gates and around to the back of the property. He parked at the bottom of a small incline. "Our plot is right over the hill."

Cindy followed him up, walking carefully in her high-heeled boots.

"That's her grave, right there." He wondered what she was thinking and feeling as she slowly walked over to the beautifully kept grave site. In warm months, there would be flowers at the base of the gravestone. Today there was a sprig of holly. He knew it had been placed there by his mother.

Cindy stared at the stone marker. Dan knew what it said by heart: OUR ANGEL, MONA ELIZABETH O'NEILL, GONE TO BE WITH THE LORD, followed by the dates of her birth and death.

Dan stayed back. Maybe he was wrong, but he felt she needed time alone.

Cindy stood looking at the grave a long time. When she finally turned, he saw that her face was streaked with tears. Her eyes slowly met his. In that moment, he realized that he had no more need to punish her.

Her punishment, which would never be over, was that she'd never known their daughter. Her memories were all about regret and sorrow, whereas his were about love and happiness.

The realization banished the last of his bitterness toward her, and for the first time since Mona's death, he felt cleansed.

They walked silently back to the car. When they arrived at the police station again, he escorted her to her rental car.

"Well," she said, standing by the open driver's-side door. "I guess this is goodbye." She pulled sunglasses out of her leather shoulder bag and put them on.

He almost smiled, remembering how she'd always worn sunglasses no matter what time of year it was.

"Thanks for being so decent," she said.

"Sorry I couldn't have given you better news."

"Yeah. Me, too." She hesitated a moment, then said, "Do you have a picture of her, Dan?"

Dan nodded, then pulled out his wallet. He removed a well-worn snapshot that showed a laughing Mona sitting on a swing, her blonde curls unruly from her exuberant play.

Cindy's throat worked as she studied the photo. "She was beautiful."

"Yes."

Reluctantly, she handed the photo back to him.

He started to return it to its place in his wallet, then stopped. "Would you like to keep this?"

"Really?"

"Yeah." What the hell, he thought. He had lots of pictures of Mona.

"Thank you, Dan."

He knew from the sound of her voice that her dark glasses hid tears. Trying to lighten the emotional moment, he said, "You leaving for Miami today?"

She shook her head. "Tomorrow."

He nodded. They stood awkwardly for a few seconds. Dan started to put out his hand and then, feeling foolish, stopped. Instead, he bent and kissed her cheek. "Take care of yourself, Cindy."

"You, too."

He stood watching until the car was out of sight. Then he slowly walked back into the station.

Glynnis didn't hear from Dan again for nearly a week. Just as she'd begun to worry and think maybe something was wrong—or that he'd changed his mind about her and decided she wasn't worth waiting for—he called and invited her and the kids to go ice-skating again.

"I thought we could skate until the kids get cold, then go have pizza somewhere."

"That sounds great."

So on Saturday afternoon they went back to the pond at Whitney Lake. It was another clear, crisp day—perfect for skating. The kids couldn't wait to get out on the ice. Livvy was so impatient she could hardly sit still long enough for Glynnis to lace up her skates.

"Livvy, if you don't stop that wiggling, you'll never get out there," Glynnis said.

"Here, let me do that," Dan said.

Glynnis couldn't believe how that little dickens of a daughter of hers immediately settled down and sat docilely while Dan finished lacing the skates.

"What can I say?" Dan said with a chuckle when he saw Glynnis's expression.

Glynnis just rolled her eyes.

Finally everyone was ready, and they skated onto the ice together.

This time, Dan did much better. He only fell once. Glynnis, trying not to laugh, bent down to help him up.

"Damned ice," he muttered. "There was a rock sticking up there. Did you see it?"

The laugh erupted. "Why don't we hold hands?"

He pretended to glare at her. "What? You think I can't stand up on my own?" Then he grinned and took her hand. Pretty soon Livvy joined them, and they put her between them. Then Michael decided he wanted to be part of the group, and he latched on to Dan's free hand.

As the four of them glided over the ice together, Glynnis realized she was happier than she'd been in a long time. She kept sneaking looks at Dan, wondering what he was thinking.

What if he got tired of waiting for her to get her act together?

What if he decided she came with too much baggage and he moved on?

The thought took the edge off her happiness, and she had to force herself to push it away.

After about an hour, Glynnis and Dan decided they'd had enough and headed for the benches, where they would sit and watch until the kids got tired, cold or hungry. Glynnis had brought a couple of thermoses of hot chocolate and poured them each a cup. They sat in companionable silence for a while.

Then, out of the blue, Dan blurted, "My ex-wife showed up at the station the other day."

Glynnis looked at him. She wasn't sure what to say.

"I'm assuming Kat told you about my ex?"

Glynnis nodded. "A little. I know she took off when your daughter was only a couple of years old."

"Yeah. Right before her second birthday, in fact. Did Kat also tell you I haven't heard from her since?"

"Yes."

"I couldn't believe she was really there. After all these years."

"How'd she know where to find you?"

"She called the Chicago PD and they told her I'd moved back to Ivy. Then she called my mother."

Glynnis was very curious, but she didn't want to overstep. As she was trying to think what she could safely ask, he started talking again.

"My mother had no sooner called to warn me that I might be hearing from Cindy when she showed up at the station." His eyes met hers. "She wanted to see Mona."

Glynnis stared at him. "Oh, no. She didn't know?"

"Nope."

"What did you say?"

"I wasn't very nice to her."

"Oh, Dan."

He heaved a sigh. "Yeah. I was pretty ashamed of myself afterward. Hell, no matter what Cindy did, nobody should hear about the death of their kid the way I told her." He looked away. "I wanted to hurt her."

Reaching over, she squeezed his arm. "You told me not to be so hard on myself. Now I'll tell you the same thing. Wanting to hurt her is a very human reaction. After all, she hurt you, didn't she?"

"She only hurt me in the context that she hurt Mona. By the time Cindy left, all I felt was good riddance."

Glynnis had wondered. Kat had insinuated as much, but hearing Dan say the words was different.

"She asked me to take her to see Mona's grave."

"Oh, Dan…"

"The reason I'm telling you all this is not to make you feel sorry for me. It's because I wanted you to know that I ended up being glad Cindy came. Seeing her, taking her out to the cemetery, it was good for me. All that anger I'd stored up over the years? It's finally gone. Thing is, I don't need to be angry anymore."

"I'm glad."

"I see things a lot more clearly."

"Good."

"You could, too, Glynnis."

She frowned, not understanding.

"You know. What you told me. About your baby."

Glynnis swallowed. "Oh."

"I think it would really help you if you could find out about her. I've done some research on it…you know, like I said I would."

"You have?"

"Yeah. There *is* a registry. It's called the International Soundex Reunion Registry. According to my information, it's the world's largest free database for relatives trying to locate each other. There are all kinds of other things you can do, too. I made a list of them, and if you like, I'll help you get started."

Glynnis hesitated. Ever since she'd told Dan about the baby, she'd wondered if she'd done the right thing. Right now, she wasn't sure, because as much as she wanted to know where her daughter was and if she was happy, she didn't want to be pushed into doing anything.

Dan quickly added, "I'm not pushing you, Glynnis. I just wanted you to know I meant what I said. I'm willing to help you whenever you're ready."

A few minutes later, Michael and Livvy announced that they were starving, and after that there was no more time for private conversation.

Things were working out okay, Dan thought. As long as he didn't see Glynnis alone, he was fine. He still wanted her—that hadn't changed—but he was able to keep things on a friendly level as long as the children were around.

He smiled. Those kids were really something. Every time he was with them, he liked them more.

Like? Be honest. You love those kids. You'd be proud to call them yours.

He'd been seeing a lot of them in the past month. Usually the four of them did something together two or three times a week. When Dan worked days, they went out for pizza or burgers at least one night during the week and Glynnis almost always invited him to come for dinner another night. They went skating and to movies on Saturdays and one Saturday, they went sledding, something Dan hadn't done since he was a kid.

Another time he'd taken them to Columbus and they'd spent the day at the aquarium. When it was warmer, they'd go to the zoo and to the beach and on picnics. Dan was thinking about buying himself a bicycle, too, because he could envision the four of them taking bike rides.

Michael was going to play T-ball this year, and Dan was looking forward to helping him with his throwing and catching and then to the games themselves.

And maybe by summer...

The thought trailed off, because Dan was at work and he knew it was best if he didn't allow himself to think about making love to Glynnis unless he was alone.

Still, the thought hovered there at the back of his mind, and he allowed himself to feel that keen edge of anticipation. Although he had never thought of himself as a patient man, he was actually enjoying stringing out the anticipation, because he was old enough to know that the end result was going to be all the sweeter for having had to wait.

Now, though, he and Glynnis were careful not to touch. Touching was dangerous because the attraction they felt for each other was strong and wouldn't be easily sublimated unless they were careful.

"Hey, Dan."

Dan looked over at Romeo.

"Wanna get some lunch?"

Dan looked at his watch. It was after twelve. "Sure. What were you thinking of?"

"You ever been to Bootsie's?"

"That the sandwich place?"

"Yeah, sandwiches and salads and soup."

"Okay, sounds good."

They pulled into Bootsie's parking lot ten minutes later. The restaurant was close to the college. Dan wondered if Glynnis ever ate there. She probably did, although she had never mentioned the place.

The restaurant was crowded. As they wove their way through the tables toward one of the empty ones at the rear, Dan suddenly saw a familiar auburn head. Even though her back was to him, he knew it was Glynnis. The woman she was with was half hidden, but just then, Glynnis moved slightly, and Dan saw that her lunch companion was Kat.

"Hey, Romeo, you go get us that table, okay? I see someone I want to say hello to."

"Okay."

Dan threaded his way through until he reached Glynnis and Kat's table. Kat saw him first and grinned.

"Hey, bro," she said.

Glynnis turned, her eyes lighting up when she saw him.

"Hello, ladies," he said, careful not to let his gaze linger on Glynnis. He gave Kat a playful punch on the arm.

"Hi, Dan," Glynnis said.

Boy, she looked good. Today, she wore a black sweater and matching slacks, and on her the color did not look sober or businesslike. It looked sexy.

"What're you doing here?" Kat asked. "I thought macho types like you wouldn't be caught dead in a place like this." She winked at Glynnis. "His normal speed is pizza or burgers."

"I know," Glynnis said. Then she blushed.

Dan knew how much she hated the way her coloring gave away her feelings, but he found her tendency to blush one of the most appealing things about her. At that moment, he wished he had the right to claim her as his. To bend down and kiss her in front of everyone. But, of course, he couldn't. He couldn't even acknowledge what she'd said in anything other than a casual way.

"Yeah, I have a tendency to eat things that are bad for me." He finally allowed his gaze to swing back to Kat, and what he saw told him that she hadn't missed much in the exchange.

"Who are you here with?" she asked now.

"My partner, Romeo Navarro. He just got us a table, so I'd better go. You guys enjoy your lunch."

"We will," Kat said.

"'Bye," Glynnis said.

"Oh, Dan, before you go, I guess we've decided to go with Antonelli's for the party."

"You have?"

"Yes. Renny consulted with Gregg, Glynnis's brother, and he says they can handle it. He gave us a really good price, too." She smiled across at Glynnis. "That's what comes of having friends in high places."

Glynnis smiled, too. "Kat was telling me about the party when you walked up."

Dan felt a little awkward because in all the times he'd been with Glynnis since the anniversary party had first been mentioned back in January, he hadn't mentioned it to her. The reason was, he wasn't sure if he wanted to ask her to go with him. He did want to, of course, but he didn't know if it was a good idea. Not unless he wanted his entire family to figure out the way things stood with him.

He was proud of himself, though. He handled the moment smoothly, simply smiling and saying, "Yeah, it's going to be great. She tell you it's a surprise?"

"Yes." Glynnis smiled. "Fifty years. Imagine."

"Well," he said, "I see Romeo's already gotten into line. I'd better go. Have fun, you two. Talk to you later."

Walking away, he knew they were talking about him.

"So who are the good-lookin' chicks?" Romeo said when Dan joined him a few minutes later. "And why didn't you introduce me?"

"The dark-haired one is my sister, and she's married."

"What about that sexy-lookin' redhead?"

"That's Mrs. March. You know. The mother of the little girl who was snatched from the mall back in December."

"Oh, yeah. I didn't recognize her. She looks different."

"You met my sister then, too."

Romeo craned his neck to look at Kat again. "Oh, yeah. She looks different, too."

"I doubt either one was at her best that night," Dan said drily.

"They're good friends, huh?"

"Yes."

They stopped talking to place their orders. While getting their drinks, Romeo brought up the subject of the two women again. "So is that March woman going with anybody?"

"Going with anybody? What do you mean?"

"C'mon, O'Neill, don't be dense. Has she got a boyfriend? Or don't you know?"

"I think she might have a boyfriend."

"Too bad. Hey, maybe I'll try my luck, anyway. Go over and say hello to her. Who knows? She might be ready for a change."

Although Dan knew a guy like Romeo wouldn't stand a chance with Glynnis, he also knew the last thing she needed was him hitting on her. "I wouldn't do that."

Romeo frowned. "Why not?"

"Because I just wouldn't."

Romeo started to say something else, then stopped. A slow smile spread across his face. "Why, Danny, *you* like her, don't you?" When Dan didn't answer, he laughed. "Yeah. You like her. Okay. I won't move in on your territory. But if you get tired of her…"

Dan ignored the gibe. That was one thing that

wasn't going to happen. He would never get tired of Glynnis.

In that moment, he decided he was going to ask her to go to the anniversary party with him. And if his family made a big deal out of it, that was fine.

Maybe it would even help things along.

He hoped so.

Because looking at her now, he knew he wasn't going to be able to wait much longer for her to be ready.

Chapter Eleven

Sabrina offered to let Michael and Livvy spend the night when Glynnis attended the anniversary party for Dan's parents.

"It's silly for you to fool with trying to find a sitter when I love having them," she said.

"But Gregg won't be around to help you, since all hands will be needed to help cater the party," Glynnis protested.

"So? It's no big deal. Besides," Sabrina said with a mischievous smile, "I'd better get in practice."

Glynnis frowned. "Practice? What do you mean?" Suddenly her eyes widened. "Sabrina! Are you pregnant again?"

Sabrina nodded. "Yes!" Her voice rang with happiness.

Glynnis threw her arms around her sister-in-law. "Oh, I'm so happy for you and Gregg. How far along are you? You're not showing."

Sabrina touched her still-flat stomach. "I know. I'm only about seven weeks. I'm due October 15th."

"I'll bet Gregg is thrilled."

Sabrina laughed. "Thrilled is an understatement. He's ecstatic."

"So am I. Oh, this is so great! What are you hoping for? Boy or girl?"

"It doesn't matter. As long as it's healthy. A boy would be nice, since we'll probably stop with two and I know Gregg would love a son, but another little girl is just fine, too. Samantha would love a sister, I'm sure." Sabrina's voice grew wistful. "I would have given anything for a sister when I was growing up." Then she smiled again. "Of course, now I have you."

Glynnis remembered how, at one time, Sabrina had thought Livvy was her sister, but that was before she'd found out Ben wasn't her biological father. Thinking about those awful days—the court battle over Ben's estate and the way Sabrina had been torn between loyalty to her mother and her love for Gregg—Glynnis was so grateful for the way things had turned out. They were lucky. She knew that. In many families, the hostilities and resentments would have caused a permanent breach, but they had managed to overcome them and build a wonderful family.

And now they would add another to their brood.

This would probably be the last baby in the family, because Glynnis didn't imagine she would be having another child, either, even if she should get married again. After all, she would be forty in just a few short months. Her childbearing days would be nearing the end.

She wondered how Dan felt about having another child. If things *did* work out between them and he asked her to marry him, would it be a problem if he couldn't have another child of his own? She knew he was crazy about Michael and Livvy, as they were about him, but would that be enough for him? Some men felt strongly about bloodlines. Maybe Dan was one of them.

And yet, if she *did* marry Dan, and he *did* want a child, her age wouldn't be the only problem to surmount. There was also the question of finances. Cops didn't make a lot of money, especially small-town cops. Glynnis probably wouldn't have the luxury of staying home with a new baby. Would she really *want* another child under those circumstances?

For the next few days, the question of having another child niggled at her. If she and Dan kept seeing each other, the subject was something they would eventually have to talk about. Whether they could come to an mutually satisfactory agreement was another question entirely.

In the meantime, she told herself, she needed to make an effort to stop putting the cart before the horse.

It took a while, but she finally managed to put the question of children out of her mind and turned her attention to the upcoming party. She was really looking forward to it. She was especially looking forward to meeting those members of Dan's family that she hadn't met through Kat. It would be interesting to see how Dan fit into the group, too. Family dynamics fascinated her, probably because she came from such a small family unit herself.

The day of the party, it snowed heavily. Glynnis drove the children over to Sabrina and Gregg's about four, then came home to start getting ready. Dan was picking her up at six-thirty.

She'd bought a new outfit for the occasion: a gorgeous amber silk crepe cocktail dress. It ended just above the knee with a slit up the front that extended to mid-thigh, three-quarter-length sleeves, and a high neckline that plunged to a deep V in the back. With it, she planned to wear high-heeled mules. She'd splurged on a brown beaded evening bag, too, even though she knew she would rarely use it after tonight. But it looked so perfect with the dress, she hadn't been able to resist.

Long sparkly gold earrings studded with rhinestones and a matching bracelet would complete her ensemble.

After pampering herself with an oil-scented bath, she dressed carefully. She'd had her hair cut the day before and wondered what Dan would think about the new do, which was much shorter than she'd worn in the past. Although initially Glynnis wasn't sure when Jenny, her longtime stylist, suggested cutting her hair shorter, now that she'd had it done, she loved it. The swingy, chin-length style made her feel younger and freer. Tonight, she'd washed and dried her hair carefully, fluffing it out the way Jenny had shown her, and Glynnis was pleased with the result.

Glynnis had also had a professional manicure and pedicure, a luxury she rarely allowed herself. But this was a special night, and she wanted to look and feel her best, even though no one but her would see her toes. Glynnis smiled. No one was going to see her underwear either, but it made her feel pretty and sexy to feel the silk and lace of her pale green panties and bra against her skin, just as she loved the feel of the gossamer thigh-high stockings she had on tonight.

Anyone would think I was planning on a night of hot sex. Just the thought of sex with Dan made her feel tingly. She knew it was dangerous to let her mind drift in that direction, but it had been so long. Just thinking about sex couldn't hurt, could it? It wasn't as if she was going to act on her thoughts.

So for a few minutes, Glynnis let herself fantasize about what it might be like to make love with Dan. She closed her eyes and imagined them coming home tonight. The house would be dark and quiet with the children gone. They would walk inside and take off their coats and gloves and boots. Standing in the entryway, he would put his arms around her and she'd slip hers around his waist. She'd look up and he'd look down. For a long moment, they'd stand there. Then slowly, he'd lower his head.

She knew just how his lips would feel. Warm and soft, then harder and more demanding as he deepened the kiss. He would taste of the wine they'd drunk and the toothpaste he'd used earlier and something else, something that was simply his essence, all male, all Dan. His hands would caress the bare skin of her back, then slip around to cup her breasts.

Her heart would thud in her ears, and when they finally drew apart, they would both be breathing hard. Desire would lie heavy between them, and silently, she would take him by the hand and lead him back to the master bedroom. Once there, she would open the blinds to allow moonlight to stream into the room, then turn to him again. They would stand there and slowly undress each other.

Her breathing became shallow as she imagined the way he would slide her dress down her shoulders. The silk would pool at her feet and shimmer in the pale light. Then she would unbutton his shirt while he unknotted his tie. Together they would unbuckle his belt and soon his clothes would join hers on the floor.

Glynnis groaned aloud as she pictured what Dan would look like clad only in his briefs. "Stop this!" she muttered, opening her eyes. "It isn't going to happen. You're just going to make yourself crazy."

Determinedly, she pushed the errant thoughts away and finished putting on her makeup. She used a shimmering bronze eye shadow and more mascara than normal. Instead of her usual neutral lipstick, she chose a glistening tangerine. When she finished, she stepped back to examine herself in the mirror. She was happy with the image she saw. Even if she couldn't indulge her earlier fantasy just yet, it was only human for her to want Dan to want her.

Laughing at herself, she picked up her evening bag, and walked out to the living room to wait for him to arrive.

Dan almost stopped breathing when he got his first look at Glynnis. She looked amazing. She was wearing a killer dress that clung to every curve and showed off legs that were pretty damned spectacular. And she'd done something to her hair. "Wow," was all he could say.

Her eyes sparkled with pleasure at the look on his face. "Thanks. You look pretty nice yourself."

Dan had bought himself a new suit, since all of his others were ones he wore to work. He'd spent a lot more money than he should have, but he hadn't been able to resist because he knew the salesman was right—the suit looked great on him. A blue so dark it was almost black, it was made from fine, light-weight wool and had needed only minor alterations. A pale gray shirt and matching gray silk tie completed his costume.

"Where are the kids?" he asked.

"Spending the night at Sabrina and Gregg's." She

slipped off her shoes and reached for her boots. "Better wear these till we get there with all that snow around."

Dan knew he was in big trouble when she turned around and he saw what she looked like from the back. Holy Moses. How would he get through the night without wrestling her to floor? Even looking at that bare, sexy expanse, he wanted to make love to her. He knew just how her skin would feel when he touched it, and how could he avoid touching it? There was going to be a band there tonight. He and Glynnis would be dancing. There'd be nowhere to put his hands without touching skin unless he put them on her bottom. Even thinking of touching her bottom made his body react. Damned good thing he had an overcoat on, he thought sheepishly.

By now, she'd finished putting on her boots and had reached for her coat. Taking it from her, he helped her into it. Smelling her fragrant hair and skin with its undertones of healthy woman, he almost said, the hell with the party, the hell with what we decided, where's the bedroom?

Down boy, down. Your problem is, you've been too long without a woman.

But Dan knew that wasn't his only problem. He didn't want just any woman. He wanted Glynnis. And he wasn't sure he could wait another day longer.

The Knights of Columbus hall looked beautiful, Glynnis thought. Dan and his siblings had done a terrific job of decorating, using greenery, gold satin bows and glittery tinsel-like gold streamers to disguise the plain walls and ceiling. They'd hung a shiny gold cloth behind the bandstand with a banner across it that read BRENDA AND MIKE, FIFTY GOLDEN YEARS.

Round tables that seated eight were dotted around the perimeter of the dance floor. A white tablecloth and a centerpiece of white and pink roses brightened every table. Kat had told Glynnis earlier that pink was the color of her mother's one attendant's dress on the day of their wedding. Lighted votive candles in crystal holders stood on each side of the flower arrangements.

When Dan and Glynnis walked in, there were already about fifty people there, and a steady stream continued to arrive. Dan's oldest brother Brian and his wife, Carolyn, would be bringing Dan's parents a little later. They would be shocked when Brian's car pulled up to the K of C hall. They thought they were going to dinner with their children. They didn't even know Shawn and Tim, who lived in Connecticut and Arizona respectively, were in town.

Dan introduced Glynnis to those members of his family she hadn't met. Soon her head was swimming, because it wasn't just his brothers and sisters and their spouses and children that were there. There were also aunts and uncles and cousins and their families.

"Heavens," she said at one point. "How do you keep them all straight?"

"It's not easy," Dan said with a laugh.

There was such a strong family resemblance. Dan's brothers Tim and Terry were just slightly younger versions of him, with the same almost-black hair and bright blue eyes. And looking at Kat's sisters, Glynnis saw the same strong genes repeated. Only Shawn, who was forty-seven to Kat's thirty-six, looked different, with lighter hair and green eyes. When Glynnis commented on the difference, Shawn said she'd been told her coloring came from her Grandmother Kelly.

Although they tried to be subtle about it, Dan's sisters gave Glynnis a close inspection. She felt self-conscious at first, then decided it was kind of flattering. She wondered what Kat had told them, for she was sure Kat had said something.

"You look terrific tonight," Kat said when Dan had gone to help one of his brothers and the two friends had a moment to talk privately. "That's a beautiful dress."

"Thanks. It cost more than I should have spent, but I hardly ever have an excuse to buy something like this, so I thought, why not?" Glynnis gave Kat an admiring glance, as well. "I love your dress, too." The sapphire blue sheath looked terrific with Kat's coloring.

Kat smiled. "You weren't the only one who spent too much, but what the heck."

Just then Shawn, who also looked gorgeous in green chiffon, walked up onto the bandstand and tapped the mic. "Hi, everybody," she said. "It's almost seven-thirty, so we're going to douse the lights soon. We'd like all of you to line up on two sides of the room. Although by the time they come inside, they'll have probably figured out what's going on, let's yell 'Surprise' anyway, okay?"

There was an excited babble as everyone scrambled to find their places and the lights were turned off. Renny, Dan's youngest sister, stood watch at the front door and would alert them when Brian's car arrived.

It didn't take long. Just a few minutes after the lights went out, Renny called out, "They're here!" A second later, she dashed into the room and took her place next to her fiancé.

Glynnis wasn't sure what had happened to Dan. She turned to look around, then suddenly he was there beside her. He put his arm around her shoulders.

Together they waited. Glynnis was very conscious of the warmth and strength of Dan's body and how good it felt to be held close to him. She'd missed more than sex since Ben died. She'd missed this, too—having someone to lean on, someone to share not just the good times but the bad. The truth was, she liked being part of a couple. And she liked Dan.

Oh, for heaven's sake, Glynnis, for once be entirely honest with yourself. You don't just like Dan. You're in love with Dan. Maybe more in love with him than you've ever been with anyone, including Ben.

The thought was sobering. For a long time, she'd justified Ben's actions and her gullibility with the belief that they had been star-crossed lovers meant to be together. But maybe that wasn't true at all. Maybe Ben had loved her because she was the antithesis of his wife and she filled that gaping hole of need with her obvious adoration and willingness to allow him to take the lead in all things. And maybe she had loved Ben because he filled her own need for a man to take charge and allow her to revert back to being the girl she was when her adored father died.

Before Glynnis could analyze and process this idea thoroughly, a stir rippled through the crowd as they heard Dan's parents enter the building. A moment later, Brenda and Mike O'Neill appeared in the doorway to the hall, along with Brian and his wife.

"Surprise!" everyone yelled. "Happy Anniversary!"

For the next ten or fifteen minutes, Glynnis and Dan were caught up in the joyful chaos. Eventually, they worked their way to where his parents stood.

Although Glynnis had been friends with Kat for nearly nine years, she'd never formally met her parents. She'd seen them in church and known who they were, but she wasn't sure they knew her at all.

Or maybe they did, she realized with a pang. She doubted there was a living soul in Ivy who hadn't heard about her bigamous marriage.

After hugging his parents, Dan took Glynnis's hand and drew her forward, saying, "Mom, Dad, I'd like you to meet my friend, Glynnis March. She's Gregg Antonelli's twin sister."

"It's a pleasure to meet you," Brenda O'Neill said. Her friendly face was wreathed in smiles. "Kat has mentioned you so many times."

"How is it a lovely lass like you has escaped my attention all these years?" Mike O'Neill said, his blue eyes twinkling.

"Now, Mike, don't you be embarrassing the girl," Brenda said. Looking at Dan, she added, "She *is* a beauty, though. I don't blame you for hiding her."

Glynnis knew she was blushing.

Dan's father laughed. "*Now* who's embarrassin' her?"

"Congratulations, Mrs. O'Neill. Mr. O'Neill," Glynnis said. "Fifty years is wonderful."

"A miracle is more like it," Dan's mother said. She winked at Glynnis.

"She's right," Dan's father said. "I'm not the easiest person in the world to live with."

"You can say that again," his wife countered.

"Once was enough," he shot back.

They all laughed.

Soon other people were waiting to convey their good wishes. As Glynnis and Dan moved away, the band struck up the opening notes to an old ballad. Glynnis couldn't place the song at first, but when Dan said, "Would you like to dance?" and they moved onto the floor, it suddenly hit her. The song was *Always* by Irving Berlin. Sure enough, the bandleader, over the opening measure, said, "Ladies and gentlemen, please join Brenda and Mike O'Neill as they dance to the song they consider theirs, *Always*."

The beautiful melody and even more beautiful words played through Glynnis's mind as Dan pulled her close. His hand, splayed across her back, sent currents of electricity through her. Was there anything more wonderful than dancing with the man you love? Glynnis wondered dreamily.

They danced seamlessly, just as if they had been dancing together all of their lives. Glynnis was surprised by how good he was. Somehow, even though he was athletic and graceful, she hadn't expected him to be an accomplished dancer. It was a wonderful surprise. Ben had not been a dancer. Not that he took her many places to find out, but a couple of times, when something Glynnis loved played on the radio or she had one of her favorite CDs on, she'd tried to coax him into dancing with her, and he'd always said, "I have two left feet." It hadn't been a big deal, but it had been a disappointment, because Glynnis had always loved to dance. So had her father. One of her earliest memories was "dancing" with her dad. He would put her feet on top of his and hum happily while they moved around the floor.

Dan was humming now, and Glynnis closed her eyes and gave herself over to the music and the feel of his body moving against hers. She remembered someone once saying that dancing is foreplay, that its movements mimic sex, and tonight she understood the truth of those statements, for once again, her body shimmered with longing. And yet the longing was almost welcome, because at least she was alive and once again feeling like a desirable woman. And she knew Dan did desire her. He didn't have to tell her so in words. She could see the desire in his eyes, and she relished the knowledge.

"You're a terrific dancer," she said when the song was over and the band began to play a faster number.

"I've got a terrific partner who's inspired me."

His smile and the look in his eyes sent a jolt of pure happiness shooting through her.

For the rest of the evening they danced almost every dance, they talked to old friends and new, they ate the wonderful food prepared by Antonelli's, they drank wine and toasted Dan's parents with champagne, they watched as the senior O'Neills opened their gifts and they unashamedly let tears fall when Brenda and Mike, at the end of the evening, danced alone to *Anniversary Waltz*.

Glynnis knew she'd never forget this night. It had been perfect in every way.

She and Dan were among the last to leave. They stayed to help his siblings load all the gifts and the leftover food into various vehicles. Finally, everything was done and Dan said, "Ready?"

Glynnis nodded.

He took her hand as they carefully made their way to his car and helped her in. It had finally stopped snowing but was bitterly cold. The car took a while to warm up. Glynnis shivered as they waited.

"I should have come out earlier and gotten it warmed before bringing you outside," Dan said.

"No, it's okay. I'm okay."

Finally, it was warm enough for him to turn on the heater. By the time they reached her house, it was actually toasty and Glynnis hated getting out. Dan pulled into the driveway and came around to the passenger side to open her door. Her foot hit a patch of ice as he helped her out, and she would have fallen if he hadn't grabbed her.

Glynnis's heartbeat quickened when, instead of letting her go, he pulled her close. Their breath puffed out as their eyes met. And then he bent his head and kissed her. As before, she was powerless to resist. None of the reasons why she shouldn't kiss him made any difference. Right now, in this place, with this man, nothing mattered except the desire that refused to be denied any longer.

The kiss went on and on. Became two kisses. Then three. It was only when he shoved his hands inside her coat and Glynnis felt them at the sides of her breasts that she was able to muster up enough awareness of just where they were to say, "Let's go inside." Her voice didn't sound like hers.

They barely made it into the house before he was kissing her again. This time she didn't try to stop him. Just as she'd fantasized, her clothes began to hit the floor. First her coat. Then his. Then her boots. Then his shoes. Then his suit jacket.

The only sounds were the quiet ticking of the grandfather clock in the corner and their ragged breathing as they kissed and touched one another greedily.

Even if Glynnis had had the strength to resist, she didn't want to. And when Dan lifted her up into his arms and murmured, "Where's your bedroom?" her only thought was how much she wanted him and damn the consequences.

Chapter Twelve

Dan's hands trembled as he helped Glynnis remove her dress. He was still a bit stunned at how fast things were happening, although from his first look at her tonight making love to her had been all he'd thought about.

And now here they were.

He told himself not to rush, to make this experience a good one for her *and* for him, but she was so beautiful and he wanted her so much. He knew it was going to be tough to keep himself under control.

Looking at her in her lacy underwear, he could feel his erection straining against his briefs. He scrambled to get his own clothes off as quickly as possible. Although she seemed shy at first, soon she was helping him. But in some ways, that made things worse, because the touch of her hands only excited him more.

She'd opened the blinds in the bedroom when they'd first come in, and moonlight striped the floor and spilled onto the bed. Standing there in the pale light, she took his breath away.

Afterwards, he never remembered whether she pulled the bedspread off the bed or they both did. He only knew that within moments, the last of the barriers between them were removed and they were twined together in bed.

Dan tried to go slow, but he was only human, and he'd been thinking about making love with Glynnis for weeks now. The feel of her skin against his, the little sounds she made when he touched her, first with his hands, then with his mouth and tongue, the way her body arched into his caress, the sweetness of her scent, the way she tasted—all combined to excite him to the point where he knew he wasn't going to be able to hold himself in much longer.

When he knew she was on the edge, he slid his fingers into her, stroking her to bring her to a quick climax, then holding her tightly as she cried as out. Only after the spasms stopped did he part her legs and raise himself up, pushing deeply into her welcoming warmth. She wrapped her legs and arms around him, digging her nails into his back as they found their rhythm and began to move together. It was excruciating to keep holding back, but he waited until he felt her body tightening around him and knew she was poised for her own climax before he finally let himself go.

His last thought before collapsing on top of her, spent and satiated, was that she was even more wonderful than he'd ever imagined.

Glynnis awoke to sunshine streaming through the opened slats of the bedroom blinds. At first, she was disoriented because she never left the blinds open when she went to bed at night. Then suddenly she remembered everything that had happened last night, and she sat bolt upright.

She stared down at Dan. He lay on his stomach, with his left leg sticking out from under the quilt. His hair was disheveled and there was a stubble of beard on his chin, but he looked gorgeous, anyway.

Flustered, her gaze drifted to the bedside clock. The digital numerals read 9:30.

Oh my God! she thought in sudden panic. *Nine-thirty! And it was Sunday and bright daylight outside.*

Scrambling out of bed, she rushed to the window. Just as she'd feared, there was Dan's car sitting smack dab in the middle of her driveway for all the world to see.

For a moment, she froze, as her mind spun frantically. Images of last night fought for dominance. The way she'd forgotten everything, especially her children, in the haze of desire that had gripped her.

Oh, my God, what had she been thinking?

Thinking? You weren't thinking. That's the problem.

She buried her hot face in her hands. She could hardly bear to remember her wanton behavior.

How many times had they made love last night? Two?

Three?

What must he think of her? After all her spouting about not being ready she'd practically thrown herself at him. Why, the dress she'd worn last night was a walking advertisement for what she wanted. How much more clear could she have made it?

"Glynnis?"

Trying to compose herself, she looked up. The smile on Dan's face and the way his gaze traveled slowly down her body was a jolting reminder that she wasn't wearing a stitch. Grabbing her robe, which hung from the bedpost, she hurriedly put it on, knotting it tightly around her.

"Now why'd you go and do that?" he drawled. "I like you much better without it." He held out his hands. "Come here, woman. Let me say good morning properly."

Glynnis's heart pounded. She shook her head. "Dan, you've got to go. Right now."

His smile faded. "Why? What's wrong?"

Oh, God. Where to start? "Your car is sitting in the driveway. The neighbors have probably already seen it." She could hear the edge of panic in her voice, even though she was trying desperately to remain calm.

He sat up abruptly, the quilt that had covered him falling away. Seeing his lean, naked chest with its sprinkling of springy, dark hair, Glynnis blushed, remembering how, last night, she had kissed her way down that chest.

Among other things.

"So?" he said.

"Dan, please. I...last night...it never should have happened. It was a mistake, and I—"

"A mistake?"

Looking at the way his eyes had gone from warm to cold in the space of seconds, Glynnis realized how what she'd said must have sounded to him. "I'm sorry, Dan, I didn't mean—" She broke off. What could she say? What had happened between them *had* been a mistake. A bad mistake.

He studied her for a moment, then swung his legs out of bed and stood facing her. He didn't bother to hide his nakedness. "Never mind. You don't have to explain. I think I know exactly what you meant. You're ashamed of what happened between us."

Oh, God. She prayed for the right words. "It's not that. I'm not ashamed. I—I just can't have the neighbors gossiping. Dan, please. Think for a minute. People already believe I'm stupid to have been taken in by Ben. I can't have them thinking I'm promiscuous, too."

"For Christ's sake, Glynnis!" he exploded. "That's the most ridiculous thing I've ever heard. It's not like you have a parade of men coming and going."

She bit her lip.

"C'mon, Glynnis. So what if one of the neighbors should see me? This is the twenty-first century, for crying out loud, not the Victorian era. I'm sure even that old biddy next door has heard of the sexual revolution."

Part of her knew he was right. But another part of her was mortified at the thought of Mrs. Hershey or holier-than-thou Sandy Fuller from across the street knowing Dan had spent the night. She could imagine what they'd say about her. What they'd think. Hadn't she heard what they'd had to say about Freda Bennington's daughter, who had been six months pregnant when she walked down the aisle?

"Please, Dan. You've got to go."

The look he gave her was withering. "You know, last night I was even thinking…" Then he shook his head. "Never mind." He bent down to pick up his briefs. Unselfconsciously, he put them on. When finished, he met her gaze again. His eyes were flat, as if he'd willed all emotion out of them. "I guess I was wrong about you." He shrugged. "Okay, I'll leave. You don't have to worry about the wrong people seeing me here. You don't have to worry about me anymore, period."

He finished dressing faster than Glynnis would have thought possible. Then, without a word, he walked out of the bedroom.

"Dan! Wait." Glynnis ran out to the hall where he

was putting on his coat. "Please don't be angry. Can…can we talk later?"

"What for? You've made yourself pretty damn clear."

"Dan, please. Try to understand."

"I do understand. Last night was a mistake, and you want me to leave." He pulled his keys out of his pocket. "I'm tired of playing games, Glynnis. You said once that you were screwed up and I said you were wrong. Well, I've changed my mind. You *are* screwed up."

He opened the front door. "I hope one of these days you figure out what the hell it is you *do* want." Without waiting for her response, he walked out, shutting the door behind him.

Glynnis stood unmoving for a long moment. But when she heard Dan's car pull out of the driveway, she ran back to the bedroom, threw herself across the bed and burst into tears.

"Geez, Dan, what've you got stuck up your ass?"

Dan glared at Romeo. "Maybe I'm just tired of stupid questions."

"Well, excuse *me* for living."

Dan knew he should apologize. Hell, it wasn't Romeo's fault that Dan was pissed off at the whole world. But he couldn't make himself say he was sorry, so the two men rode in silence for the remainder of their trip. They were on their way to question a witness to a burglary that had taken place an hour earlier.

Dan let Romeo take the lead when they arrived at the liquor store on the northwest edge of Ivy. It was his own way of apologizing to Romeo and seemed to work, because when they'd finished with the witness and were on their way back to the station, Romeo was whistling.

Dan didn't recognize the tune, but that didn't surprise him. He didn't listen to much contemporary music.

He tried to empty his mind or, at the very least, to think about Jack's visit, which was finally taking place on the coming weekend. But his mind wasn't cooperating. It had been nine days now since he'd stalked out of Glynnis's house, and he hadn't talked to or seen her since. Several times, he'd almost called her, but each time he decided the next move was up to her. So far, she hadn't made one.

Face it, he told himself. *She's a total mess, and she doesn't know what she wants. She blows hot and cold and if you keep going back for more, you deserve whatever you get. Better to suck it up now and get her out of your system before you get in any deeper.*

Kat had been right all along.

Why hadn't he listened to her?

"Mom, what's Dan's number?"

Glynnis jumped, and spaghetti sauce from the spoon she held splattered onto the stove. She'd been so lost in her thoughts she hadn't heard Michael come into the kitchen. "His telephone number, you mean?" It was unbelievable how much it hurt just to hear Dan's name spoken aloud.

"Uh-huh."

Wiping up the spill, she said, "Um, Michael, why do you want to call Dan?"

"'Cause he promised we'd practice playing catch before T-ball starts. And he hasn't come."

This last was said with an indignant frown, which wasn't at all like Michael.

Glynnis forced her voice to sound upbeat. "Well, honey, he's probably really busy. Police officers have to work hard, you know."

"But Mom, he *promised*."

"I know he promised, Michael, but sometimes grown-ups make promises that they can't keep. I'm sure he'll come if he can."

"But why can't I *call* him?"

Glynnis studied her unhappy son's face while she chose what words to use. "Because calling him wouldn't be polite. I told you, Michael. He'll come if he can. And if he can't, I don't want you bugging him."

"I'm not going to bug him. I just want to ask him when he's coming."

Michael was so well-behaved most of the time that Glynnis tended to forget that, like his sister, he also had a stubborn streak and could dig in his heels with the best of them. It was obvious reasoning wasn't going to work. Glynnis knew this time she'd have to be firm.

"The answer is no, Michael, you can't call him. Now I don't want to hear another word about this." She turned back to the sauce.

"You're *mean!* I hate you!"

Glynnis was so shocked, she dropped the spoon and spun around. Michael had already raced out of the kitchen, and she could hear him crying as he headed for his room.

Telling herself not to overreact, she went after him. When she reached the doorway to his room, she saw him huddled on the bed. His shoulders were shaking. She was very glad Olivia was on a play date with one of her little day care buddies. "Michael," she said gently. "I'm sorry you're so upset with me. I love you, honey. I'm not trying to be mean." She sat on the bed and rubbed his shoulders.

At her words, he just cried harder.

It hurt Glynnis to look at him. Poor little tyke. He'd been through so much in his short life. He'd not only lost his father, he'd had to endure some teasing from other children, and that had been hard on him. Glynnis vividly remembered the day he came home from school sobbing because some classmate had taunted him, saying, "My mother said your father was a bad man."

She also remembered how he'd started wetting the bed after Ben died. It had taken almost a year for him to sleep through the night without an accident, and it was only this year, in second grade, that he'd seemed to have gone back to being the well-adjusted, sweet boy he'd started out to be.

At that moment, Glynnis didn't blame Michael if he hated her. She hated herself! She'd known how unfair it was to introduce a man into Michael's life if the man wasn't someone who would be there permanently. She knew how careful she had to be. She knew she had to be darned sure she kept her relationship with Dan one of friendship only, that anything else would be grossly unfair—not only to her children but to Dan himself.

And look what she'd done!

Why was she so weak?

Why did she keep making mistake after mistake?

You don't deserve these children.

"Michael, sweetheart, won't you look at me?" Glynnis was on the verge of tears herself. She continued to stroke his back, and finally he stopped crying.

With a deep shudder, he turned over and sat up. He wouldn't look at her, though.

"I'm sorry, sweetie," she said again. "I should have been honest with you."

That got his full attention.

Glynnis ached at the sight of his tear-stained face when he turned it toward her. "The truth is, Dan and I...we had a disagreement. Dan is angry with me. That's why he hasn't been coming over."

Michael frowned. "He's angry with you?"

"Yes."

He considered this. "But he's not angry with me."

"No."

"Then why can't I call him?"

Glynnis sighed. "Because it would make Dan feel bad if you called. Tell you what. We'll call cousin Steve and ask him if he'll come over and play catch with you. You know he used to be a really good baseball player, don't you?"

"Yeah."

"Well, I'm sure he'd love to play with you."

Michael said nothing, just stared at her with his big eyes. Finally, he shrugged. "I guess that'd be okay."

Glynnis knew he was still unhappy, but there was nothing she could do about it. It would be cowardly to allow him to call Dan, because she knew Dan would never turn Michael down. But if Dan came back, it had to be because he wanted to be with her, not because he felt bad about Michael.

So no matter how unhappy Michael was about the present situation, it wasn't going to change. Not until Glynnis figured out exactly what it was she wanted and was ready to take the next step. Even then, maybe nothing would change. Maybe Dan no longer had any desire to be with her.

For all she knew, her insecurities and problems had driven Dan away for good.

Dan was surprised when Kat called and asked him to meet her for lunch. "It'll have to be quick," he said, looking at his watch. "I've got a court appearance at one."

"How about Columbo's Pizza?"

"Okay."

"I can be there in fifteen minutes."

"See you then."

As he drove to the popular restaurant, Dan wondered why Kat had called him. He knew she had a reason, because she never just called.

He didn't have to wait long to find out. They'd no sooner placed their order for a large mushroom/sausage pizza than she plunged right in.

"What's wrong between you and Glynnis?" she asked. She squeezed lemon into her Diet Coke and took a long swallow.

"Why do you ask?" he hedged.

"C'mon, Dan, I know you didn't pay any attention to my warning and that you've been seeing her steadily. I also know you no longer are because I asked her point-blank. So something happened, because the night of the party it was obvious to all of us that the two of you were crazy about each other."

"Yeah, well, looks can be deceiving."

Her eyes widened. "You're saying you *don't* have feelings for her?"

"Maybe she doesn't have feelings for me."

Kat just stared at him. "All right, now I know something happened. C'mon. Talk to me."

Dan shrugged. "I'm sorry, Kat, but I don't want to talk about it, okay? Let's just say things didn't work out." There was no way he was going to tell her about that night, sister or no sister. Some things were too private to discuss. Hell, he didn't ask Kat about *her* sex life.

Kat leaned forward. "Dan, listen to me. I saw Glynnis last night, and if ever anyone was miserable, she is. But she wouldn't talk about what was wrong, either." She heaved a sigh. "And it's not just her that's suffering from whatever it is that happened. Michael mentioned you twice and it was clear he misses you and is confused about why you've stopped coming around. Even Livvy talked about you."

That made Dan feel bad. He missed the kids, too.

"Dan," Kat said softly, "I was wrong before. I see that now. And whatever it is that's happened between you, I'd like to help. Talk to me."

"Nobody asked for your help."

"Well, it's pretty damned obvious that the two of you *need* it. I mean, how bad can things be? Whatever happened between you can't be that impossible to work out, can it?"

He shook his head. "You don't understand."

"How could I? You won't talk to me. But I do know one thing, Dan. When things happen between people who love one another, they don't let pride get in their way."

For the rest of the day, Dan thought about what Kat had said. Kat was right. He loved Glynnis. He was miserable without her. And he *was* letting pride get in the way of working things out.

Glynnis had just put the children to bed and was looking forward to another lonely evening of second-guessing herself and missing Dan when the doorbell rang.

Her heart nearly stopped when she looked out and saw Dan on the doorstep. Fumbling with the lock, she finally managed to get the door open.

"Hello, Glynnis."

"H-hi." For the life of her, she couldn't get another word out. She had been so miserable for so many days now, and so tired of putting on a cheerful face for her colleagues, her students, her friends and her family that she was an emotional wreck, only inches away from falling apart.

"May I come in?"

"Oh, of course. I'm sorry." She stood back. He looked so serious.

"Are the kids in bed?" he said as he walked past her into the hallway.

"Yes." She shut the door and leaned against it. Her heart was beating so fast and so hard, she was sure he could hear it.

He took off his leather jacket and hung it on the clothes tree. Under it, he wore a black sweater and jeans. He looked wonderful. Glynnis could just imagine how *she* looked in an old pair of corduroy pants, a faded sweatshirt and no makeup.

"Can we go in the living room?" he asked.

"Of course. Do…can I get you something to drink?" She knew she sounded stiff and unwelcoming, but she couldn't relax. Not until she knew why he was here. If only he'd smile, then maybe she'd have some idea of what was coming, but so far he'd been completely somber.

"No, thanks. Can we just talk?"

"Of course." Oh, Lord, how many times had she said that now? She led the way into the living room.

"Look, I'm not going to beat around the bush," he said, waving away her invitation to sit. "I just wanted to tell you something and ask you a question."

Glynnis, who hadn't taken a seat, either, was afraid to hope.

He put his hands on her shoulders and searched her eyes for what seemed an eternity. "I love you," he said gruffly. "And I need to know if you love me."

For a moment, Glynnis couldn't believe what she'd heard. She'd been so prepared for something bad, so sure he was going to say he'd given it a lot of thought and realized things would never work out between them, but couldn't they still be friends, or something similar, that what he'd really said took a while to sink in. When it did, tears sprang into her eyes. "Oh, Dan." Her voice shook. "Y-yes, I love you, but I…" She took a deep breath and drew back so she could see his face. It was time for total honesty between them. "I feel I don't deserve you. I don't deserve to be happy."

"Ah, Glynnis, that's not true. Everyone deserves to be happy. Why would you say such a thing, anyway?"

"Isn't it obvious? I've…I've made a total mess of my life." *Every man I've ever loved has left me.* At the thought, Glynnis froze. That was it. That was what had been eating at her for a long, long time. Why hadn't she realized it before?

"What is it?" Dan said.

Glynnis licked her lips. "I suddenly realized something. Why…I've been so afraid."

"Tell me."

She swallowed. Could she? Could she admit the real reason she'd driven him away?

"C'mon, Glynnis. Don't shut me out. Whatever it is, you can tell me."

She took a deep breath for courage. "Every man I've ever loved has left me. Down deep, I think I've always felt their leaving was my fault. That if I'd been a better person, more deserving, they wouldn't have left. And…I guess I was afraid the same thing would happen with you." Now she couldn't stop the tears. Saying her worst fears had unleashed something inside her. "And my children would suffer again, just like they had in the past." The tears were a flood now, but she had to get it all out. "That's the worst part. Knowing I've made my children suffer."

"Glynnis…" He forced her chin up and looked deep into her eyes. "Listen to me. I am not that jerk you fell for in college, and I am not Ben. When I love someone, I stick by them, and I love you. I love your kids, too. I am not going to leave you. Sure, we've got some things to work out, but we'll work them out together. Understand?"

She nodded.

"Say it."

"I—I understand."

He gave her another long, searching look. Finally he smiled. And then he lowered his mouth to hers, and for a long time, there was no more talk between them.

Chapter Thirteen

"So now I just wait?"

Dan leaned over and kissed her cheek. "Now you just wait."

Glynnis sighed. The two of them were in her home office, which had originally belonged to Ben. Once she had decided she was going to take Dan's advice and find the daughter she'd given up almost twenty years ago, she'd invested in a new, state-of-the-art computer. She'd even splurged for one of those thin, flat screens.

It was just a week since Dan had told her he loved her, but so much had happened since. They'd had a long, long talk that same night, and Glynnis had finally agreed with Dan that it wasn't enough to know why she felt the way she did; she had to take action to change. She had promised him two things that night. The first was that she would get the counseling she had always denied she needed, and the second was that she would try to find her daughter. She knew now that both things were necessary, or she would never be able to put the past behind her and move on.

The very next day, she'd begun.

She'd asked around and been given the name of a family therapist who had an excellent reputation. She had an appointment to see Dr. Faron in two days.

She'd also begun the search for her daughter. As Dan had suggested once before, she started by registering with the International Soundex Reunion Registry. With Dan's help, she also searched the Internet and found several helpful Web sites that gave step-by-step procedures to follow if you were trying to find your child or vice versa.

She researched California adoption laws, then registered with several free databases that concentrated on California adoptions.

"There *is* one other thing you can try," Dan said after reading an article on adoptee reunions with their birth parents. "And that's contact the clinic where you gave birth."

Glynnis couldn't believe she hadn't thought of that herself. She glanced at her watch. It was seven o'clock, which meant it was four o'clock in California. "I'm going to call them right now."

Five minutes later, armed with the number, she placed the call. When the call was answered, she asked for the office of the director.

"Mrs. Ashley's office," a pleasant female voice said a few seconds later.

"Hi. My name is Glynnis Antonelli and I gave birth to a daughter at your clinic twenty years ago. I placed her for adoption, and now I'm trying to find her. Can you help me?"

"Let me connect you with Miss Sloan. She handles all search questions."

"Thank you." Glynnis looked at Dan, who gave her a reassuring smile.

A few moments later, another, younger, female voice said, "This is Valerie Sloan."

"Miss Sloan?" Glynnis repeated her request.

"I'll see what I can do to help you," Valerie Sloan said. "What is your daughter's birth date?"

Glynnis told her both date and time of birth and spelled her last name.

"We computerized everything a couple of years ago, so if your daughter has made any inquiries about you, it will only take a few minutes for me to get that information. If she hasn't, you can give me your contact information, and we'll register you. That way, if she ever *does* come to us looking for you, we can send her in the right direction."

"Thank you," Glynnis said. She could hear the Sloan woman clicking computer keys while she waited. Her heart started beating faster, and she reached for Dan's hand. *She's looking,* she mouthed. He squeezed her hand in support.

"Sorry to be taking so long," Valerie Sloan said after a couple of minutes. "The computer is slow today."

"That's okay." Of course, with every second gone by, Glynnis became more nervous.

"Ms. Antonelli?"

"Yes?"

"Our records show that your daughter has indicated she would like to locate you."

Goose bumps broke out on Glynnis's arms.

"Ms. Antonelli? Did you hear me?"

Glynnis took a deep breath. "Yes, sorry. I—I was just so stunned for a moment. What…what do we do now?"

"Now you give me your address and phone number. I will call your daughter and tell her you've contacted us and that you're agreeable to her calling you."

"I can't call her?"

"No, I'm afraid not. That's not the way we work. She has to be the one to make the first move."

So Glynnis gave the woman everything she wanted. She also agreed to fax the clinic proof of her identity, including copies of her driver's license, social security card and the original birth certificate of her daughter.

"That's to protect everyone," Valerie Sloan said. "We want to make absolutely sure you're who you say you are."

"I understand."

When Glynnis disconnected the call, she was trembling inside. "Oh, Dan," she said. "They said she had contacted them. That she wants to find me."

"That's great!"

Glynnis took a long, shaky breath. "I know. But it's also scary." She closed her eyes. "What if she hates me?"

"Glynnis, stop that. I don't think she'd be trying to find you if she hated you."

"I wouldn't blame her if she did."

"Man, I sure am glad you're seeing that shrink on Tuesday."

After a moment, Glynnis laughed. "I need to, don't I?"

"Yes, you do."

"Oh, Dan." She reached for him, and he enfolded her in his arms. "I'm so mixed up. Happy and scared and hopeful."

"I know." He rubbed her back.

"Without you, I'm not sure I would have done this."

"Sure you would. It might have taken you longer, but in the end, you'd have done it."

"What makes you so sure?"

"Because you're a lot stronger and tougher than you think you are, Glynnis. You're always beating up on yourself, but look at what you've accomplished. You had a baby and gave her up for adoption, which took a lot of strength. Then you finished college, got your master's degree, and built a good career for yourself. And when Ben died, and you found out how he'd lied to you, you didn't fall apart. You held your head up and you were strong for your kids. No matter what's happened to you in your life, you've carried on."

Glynnis thought about what he'd said. He was right. She *was* strong. She could do this. She could face her daughter. She *needed* to face her daughter. And no matter what happened, good or bad, she would carry on. She smiled at Dan. "I'm so lucky to have you."

He grinned. "And don't you ever forget it."

Glynnis hugged Dan. "I'm so nervous."

"Are you sure you don't want me to go with you?"

They were standing just outside the security checkpoint at the Ivy Regional Airport. Glynnis was taking a puddle jumper to Columbus and then flying on to L.A., where she would be meeting her firstborn daughter.

"I wish I could have you with me, but I know this is something I have to do by myself."

Dan kissed the tip of her nose. "Have a safe flight, and call me when you get there."

"I will."

They kissed again, then Glynnis waved goodbye and headed for the security check.

Fifty minutes later, she was buckling her seat belt. An hour after that, she was headed for her gate in Columbus. Finally, three hours and forty minutes after leaving her house, she was installed in the window seat of row ten of the 737 winging her on her way to L.A.

She still couldn't believe she was really going to be seeing her daughter in the space of hours.

Hope Marguerite Hudson.

Glynnis kept whispering the name to herself. It still humbled her to know that Hope's adoptive parents had kept the name Glynnis had entered on the birth certificate. Glynnis had never even allowed herself to *think* the name because to do so would have made her loss even more painful than it was.

The Marguerite came from Hope's adoptive mother, Hope had explained in that first tentative phone call. The phone call that Glynnis had feared would never come, for an excruciating eight days went by before Hope contacted her.

She'd apologized, saying she and her father had been away. "He had to go to London on business, and luckily for me, the trip coincided with spring break, so I joined him."

Just remembering how poised and confident Hope had sounded sent a surge of pride through Glynnis.

They had only talked about fifteen minutes that first time, exchanging pertinent information and not much else. Glynnis had learned that Hope's adoptive mother—the aforementioned Marguerite—had died five years earlier of a particularly virulent form of leukemia and that Hope's adoptive father, whose name was Brad, was a financial whiz who owned his own investment firm and worked mainly with large trusts.

During that initial contact, Hope didn't ask why Glynnis had given her up for adoption. Nor did she ask about her birth father. But Glynnis knew that was only a matter of time. She'd already decided she was going to be completely honest with Hope. The girl deserved nothing less.

Hope did tell Glynnis what prompted her to begin looking for her origins. She said that after her mother died, she had started thinking about genetics and health risks and had realized she needed to know about her own genetic background so that she would be better informed for the day when she might marry and have children.

After the call ended, Glynnis had felt a mixture of happiness tempered with caution and a need to protect herself. She knew she had to be prepared in case all Hope *ever* wanted from her was medical and genetic information.

But then Hope called her again the next day. And the next. Gradually, Hope had asked questions about Glynnis's life and talked about her own life. Glynnis learned that Hope was an art major. This disclosure caused Glynnis to have such a huge lump in her throat she could hardly speak for moments afterward. She'd also learned that Hope loved to swim and had been on the swim team in high school. And that she was a golfer.

"One of my passions." She laughed, then said proudly, "My dad is a terrific golfer. So good he could have turned pro. He taught me to play."

It was bittersweet for Glynnis to hear the love and admiration in Hope's voice when she talked about her adoptive father. She would always be thankful that Hope had had such wonderful parents and that she was so close to her father, but she also realized anew all that she'd missed, because Hope was obviously a terrific young woman.

Hope now knew about Michael and Livvy, and she'd asked Glynnis to e-mail pictures of them, which Glynnis had done. Hope had immediately called Glynnis afterward. There'd been a catch in her voice when she'd talked about the children. "I have red hair, too," she said.

Glynnis's eyes had filled with tears. They'd said goodbye soon after. Both had been too emotional to talk long. But the next day they'd sent pictures of each other via e-mail. Glynnis *did* cry when she saw Hope's picture. She was a lovely young woman, with serious-looking blue eyes—Philip had had blue eyes—and, as she'd said, Glynnis's red hair. The funny thing was, except for the red hair, she looked like Gregg, and Glynnis didn't look like him at all.

Seeing Hope's photo had only made Glynnis want to see her in person.

And now—Glynnis looked at her watch—in just a bit over two hours, she would.

For the remainder of the flight, Glynnis tried to

read, but found it impossible. The minutes seemed to drag by, but finally they were parking at the gate and it was time to exit through the Jetway. Hope and her father were meeting Glynnis down in baggage claim, since new security measures prohibited them from coming to the gate.

Glynnis had told Hope she'd be easy to spot. "I'll be wearing a yellow blazer and carrying a cherry-red tote. And, of course, there's my red hair."

"Yellow's my favorite color," Hope had said shyly. Then, gifting Glynnis with a dash of pure happiness, she added, "I'll wear yellow, too."

When Glynnis arrived at baggage claim, she headed straight for her carousel because she knew that's where Hope and her father would most likely be. When she got there, the first two people she saw were a tall, slender, auburn-haired girl in a yellow sweater and blue jeans, accompanied by a good-looking, dark-haired man standing protectively close.

Hope smiled tentatively, then glanced up at her father. He gave her an encouraging nod, and she walked toward Glynnis, who was incapable of moving herself. *My baby is so beautiful.*

"Hi," Hope said, stopping in front of Glynnis.

"Hi." Glynnis told herself not to cry—the last thing she wanted was to make Hope or her father uncomfortable—but she was so close to coming undone that she was afraid she wouldn't be able to stop herself. "You…you're so beautiful."

"Thank you." Hope smiled. "You look just like your picture."

They stood awkwardly for a few moments. Then Glynnis got up her courage. "Would you mind if I hugged you?"

"No, I—I'd like that."

When Glynnis put her arms around Hope, the knowledge that this warm and lovely girl was flesh of her flesh and bone of her bone, something inside Glynnis finally gave way and she knew the emptiness and pain she'd carried within for so long would finally be gone.

Later, when she told Dan about the day, she couldn't describe her emotions. They were too tumultuous. Too much happened in too short a time. It would take Glynnis a while to absorb everything and to fully realize that a day she'd dreamed about for such a long time had actually taken place.

After hugging and meeting Brad Hudson, who was quietly reserved but someone Glynnis immediately knew she would like, they retrieved Glynnis's suitcase from the carousel and headed for the parking lot.

The drive from the airport to the house where Hope had grown up and still lived took almost an hour and a half because of the notorious L.A. traffic. Located in Dana Point in Orange County, it sat high on a hill with an ocean view, but was otherwise unpretentious. In fact, it was homey and warm and filled with comfortable-looking furniture and lots of family photos.

Glynnis had planned to stay in a motel—in fact had made a reservation—but Brad Hudson would not hear of it. "We have a guest room, and both Hope and I would like for you to stay with us."

After unpacking and freshening up, Glynnis joined Hope and her father on the partially covered, brick-walled patio upon which deep purple bougain-villea grew in riotous profusion. A fat tiger-striped cat, which at first Glynnis thought was ornamental but turned out to be alive, snoozed in a sunny corner.

Hope and Brad sat at a glass-topped table with glasses of iced tea in front of them. A pitcher of tea and a plate of what looked like homemade sugar cookies was also on the table, along with napkins, wedges of lemon, sugar and long-handled spoons.

"This is lovely," Glynnis said, looking out at the view. The ocean sparkled under the late afternoon sun and dozens of sailboats dotted its surface. "You have a fantastic view."

Brad Hudson smiled. "Yes. It's what sold Hope's mother and I on the house...and what's kept us here so long." He gave Hope a fond look. "It was a good place to raise Hope." Then he turned his brown eyes to Glynnis. "I've wanted to say something to you for many years. In fact, I've said this to you mentally for a long time."

Glynnis's eyes were riveted to his.

"I just wanted to thank you for giving us such a precious gift." He reached for Hope's hand. "I know it took courage. Just know that what you did was the most wonderful thing anyone could ever do for another person."

And with that, the last remnant of regret that Glynnis might have felt disappeared, too, down the same path the pain had gone earlier. With its passing, Glynnis knew she was well on her way to becoming a whole person again, a person ready for the next stage of her life, a person worthy of the love of the man who waited at home for her return.

The rest of her visit seemed to fly by. Hope proudly showed her all the places that had been or still were important in her life: where she went to church, where her elementary school had been, where she'd attended high school and even where her mother was buried.

Throughout, they seemed more like two women who were learning to become friends more than mother and daughter, but that was all right, Glynnis thought. That was more than all right. She didn't expect more. Hope had made it clear from the very first that she already had a mother and a father that she loved. She wasn't looking for a replacement.

It wasn't until Glynnis's last night with them, after Brad had excused himself and gone to bed, and Glynnis and Hope were still sitting outdoors, that Hope finally asked about Philip.

"I don't want to meet him," she said. "I just want to know who he is and…and what happened. That is, if you want to tell me."

So Glynnis did. She told Hope everything, holding nothing back, not even the things that shamed her, because Hope deserved the truth.

Hope listened quietly. When Glynnis had finished, they sat silently for a long time. Then very softly, Hope said, "Thank you for telling me."

Glynnis nodded. "I know you said you don't want to meet him, but wouldn't you like to have his family's medical history? It could be important."

"I don't know. I'll have to think about it."

"I haven't kept tabs on him. I'm not sure if he is even still teaching. He was a good bit older than me, you know. In fact, he's probably in his mid-sixties now. He may be retired." Or he may be dead, she thought.

"I'll think about it," Hope said again.

Glynnis decided she might check into Philip Van Horne's whereabouts, anyway. She didn't have to take any action. She certainly wouldn't contact him, but it might be useful to have the information in case Hope ever did decide she wanted it.

The next day, she was sorry to say goodbye, but she felt good about the visit and about Hope and her circumstances. The girl had a very good life, and that life had been given to her by Glynnis. Glynnis could be proud of that, as well as proud of the woman Hope had become.

At the airport, Hope promised to keep in touch. At the very last moment, Glynnis said, "If you ever want to come to Ivy and meet the children, you will always be welcome."

"Thank you."

When it was time for Glynnis to go, she and Brad shook hands, she and Hope hugged hard, final good-byes were said, and then Glynnis forced herself to smile and wave and walk away.

"Damn, but I missed you!" Dan said. He grabbed her and twirled her around.

"Put me down, you nut!" But Glynnis was laughing. She could hardly wait to begin telling him everything that had happened since the last time they'd talked.

She waited until they'd collected her suitcase before beginning. She talked all the way home and was still talking when they pulled into Gregg and Sabrina's driveway. Then she had to repeat a lot of it because Gregg and Sabrina wanted to hear everything, too.

By the time she and Dan had taken the children home and gotten them into bed, and finally had time to themselves, Glynnis was all talked out. She wanted nothing more than to relax: to take her shoes off and sink down on the couch with a glass of wine and Dan beside her.

So when Dan said, "Glynnis, we need to talk," she moaned.

"Can't it wait until tomorrow?"

"No, this is too important."

Glynnis frowned. He sounded so serious. Had something happened? Something he hadn't wanted to tell her until she was home? A nugget of fear knotted in her stomach.

Dan put his glass of wine on the coffee table. Completely shocking Glynnis, he knelt in front of her. Taking her wineglass, he put it next to his on the coffee table. Then he took her hand. "They say this is the way it's done," he said, grinning. Then in a mock-serious tone belied by the love shining in his eyes, he said, "Glynnis Antonelli, will you do me the honor of becoming my wife?"

As if on cue, Glynnis began to cry.

"Damn, woman," he said, getting up and sitting next to her. "You cry more than anyone I know." He put his arm around her. "Don't you *want* to marry me?"

"Oh, Dan." It was all she could say.

He kissed her then—a long, sweet, wonderful kiss that made everything in her sing with happiness. When he finally let her up for air, she sighed. "I want to marry you more than anything in the world."

"So I take it that's a yes?" he said with a chuckle.

"Yes!" she cried. "Yes, yes, yes."

This time when they kissed, Glynnis knew she'd finally gotten it right. Dan wasn't just the man of the hour. He was a man for forever.

Five years later...

"Stop wiggling, Livvy. Now do you remember what you're supposed to do?" Glynnis straightened the ring of flowers circling Livvy's head for at least the tenth time.

Livvy made a face. "I'm supposed to walk down

the aisle like Miss Penny showed me, and I'm supposed to throw these petals on the carpet so Hope can walk on 'em."

Glynnis prayed her feisty eight-year-old would actually *do* what she'd been taught, but with Livvy, you never knew. "All right, sweetheart, I have to go sit with Dan and Michael and Danny now, but I'm counting on you to do a good job for your sister."

Livvy rolled her eyes. "I will, Mom," she said with exaggerated patience.

Glynnis patted Livvy's head, gave Penny Carstairs, the wedding coordinator, a look that said, *You'll keep her in line, won't you?* and then quickly made her way down the aisle to where Dan and Michael and their two-year-old—the son Glynnis considered her miracle since she was forty-three when he was born, along with Sabrina and Gregg and their two children—who all sat one row behind the Hudson family.

Her eyes misted as she looked around her. To think she was really here attending her daughter's wedding. So many wonderful things had happened between her and Hope over the past five years. Their relationship had deepened to the point where there was no longer any awkwardness between them. They could—and did—talk about everything. Hope had visited Ivy several times, and Dan and Glynnis and the children had gone to California at least once a year. Glynnis knew she would never take the place of Marguerite, but she had carved her own place in

Hope's life, and for this and all her other blessings, she thanked God nightly.

"You okay?" Dan whispered.

Afraid she'd cry—he was always accusing her of crying at the drop of a hat!—she just nodded and reached for his hand.

A few moments later, the first strains of *Trumpet Voluntary* sounded on the organ. The crowd stirred as one, everyone turning to get their first glimpse of the wedding party.

Glynnis watched through a blur of tears as the four young women who were Hope's bridesmaids did the hesitation walk down the aisle in their pale yellow lace dresses, followed by Camille Storey, Hope's former college roommate and maid of honor. Camille, a statuesque blonde, looked gorgeous in seafoam green.

Then came Livvy. Her red curls were piled on top of her head, around which the ring of yellow roses tipped alarmingly again. Her yellow dress looked adorable on her, though, and the lump in Glynnis's throat grew as she watched her youngest daughter solemnly and carefully throwing down her rose petals exactly as she'd been taught.

And then, finally, came the bride.

Glynnis couldn't stop the tears now. Seeing Hope in her beautiful satin gown, her red hair glowing under her veil, going to meet Josh Scanlon, the love of her life, on the arm of a beaming Brad, was the stuff of fairy tales.

Dan put his arm around her, and Glynnis leaned into his loving support. He knew what she was feeling. He always knew what she was feeling. If Glynnis hoped for anything that day, it was that Hope would find with Josh the kind of relationship Glynnis had found with Dan.

She watched through her tears as Brad and Hope reached the altar. The scent of roses mingled with the smoke of all the candles, and the lowering sun shone through the stained glass windows, casting jewel tones over the assembled guests.

"Who gives this woman to be married to this man?" the minister asked.

"Her mother and I do," Brad said.

Then, in a moment that would forever be etched in her mind, he turned and smiled at Glynnis, beckoning for her to join him.

As if in a dream, Glynnis stood. Before walking to join Brad and Hope, she glanced down at Dan, who held Danny on his lap.

Their eyes locked. She remembered how he'd once told her she deserved to be happy.

Heart full, she finally believed it was true.

* * * * *

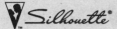

SPECIAL EDITION™

Coming in September 2004
from beloved author

ALLISON LEIGH

MEN OF THE DOUBLE C RANCH

Home on the Ranch

(Silhouette Special Edition #1633)

When his daughter suffered a riding
accident, reclusive rancher Cage Buchanan
vowed to do anything to mend his daughter's
broken body and spirit. Even if that promise
meant hiring his enemy's daughter, Belle Day.
And though Cage thought Belle was the last
person he needed in his life, she drew him
like a moth to a flame....

Available at your favorite retail outlet.

If you enjoyed what you just read,
then we've got an offer you can't resist!

Take 2 bestselling
love stories FREE!

Plus get a FREE surprise gift!

Clip this page and mail it to Silhouette Reader Service™

IN U.S.A.	IN CANADA
3010 Walden Ave.	P.O. Box 609
P.O. Box 1867	Fort Erie, Ontario
Buffalo, N.Y. 14240-1867	L2A 5X3

YES! Please send me 2 free Silhouette Special Edition® novels and my free surprise gift. After receiving them, if I don't wish to receive anymore, I can return the shipping statement marked cancel. If I don't cancel, I will receive 6 brand-new novels every month, before they're available in stores! In the U.S.A., bill me at the bargain price of $4.24 plus 25¢ shipping and handling per book and applicable sales tax, if any*. In Canada, bill me at the bargain price of $4.99 plus 25¢ shipping and handling per book and applicable taxes**. That's the complete price and a savings of at least 10% off the cover prices—what a great deal! I understand that accepting the 2 free books and gift places me under no obligation ever to buy any books. I can always return a shipment and cancel at any time. Even if I never buy another book from Silhouette, the 2 free books and gift are mine to keep forever.

235 SDN DZ9D
335 SDN DZ9E

Name	(PLEASE PRINT)	
Address	Apt.#	
City	State/Prov.	Zip/Postal Code

Not valid to current Silhouette Special Edition® subscribers.

Want to try two free books from another series?
Call 1-800-873-8635 or visit www.morefreebooks.com.

* Terms and prices subject to change without notice. Sales tax applicable in N.Y.
** Canadian residents will be charged applicable provincial taxes and GST.
All orders subject to approval. Offer limited to one per household.
® are registered trademarks owned and used by the trademark owner and or its licensee.

SPED04R   ©2004 Harlequin Enterprises Limited

**Fascinating and irresistible,
the mysterious Donovan cousins are back!**

#1 *New York Times* bestselling author

NORA ROBERTS

Readers met Nash Kirkland in *Captivated* and Sebastian Donovan in
Entranced. Now don't miss Anastasia and Liam's stories in *Charmed*
and *Enchanted*—two stories about the magical power of love.

Charmed and Enchanted

Available in September 2004

Where love comes alive™

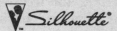

SPECIAL EDITION™

Book Three in the exciting saga of

THE PARKS EMPIRE

Dark secrets. Old lies. New loves.

The Rich Man's Son

(Silhouette Special Edition #1634)
Coming in September 2004

from reader favorite

JUDY DUARTE

When angry young Rowan Parks tries to flee his
present after a fight with his father, he ends up in
a bad accident and loses his past—to amnesia!
Unable to recall anything about what he was
running from—or to—he accepts help from beautiful
Louanne Brown, a local rancher and single mom
struggling to make ends meet. What Rowan
doesn't know is that Louanne is also trying to hide
from an evil threat—and as they begin to fall for
each other, the danger puts their future at risk!

Available at your favorite retail outlet.

**The *New York Times* bestselling author of
16 Lighthouse Road and *311 Pelican Court*
welcomes you back to Cedar Cove,
where life and love is anything but ordinary!**

DEBBIE MACOMBER

Dear Reader,

I love living in Cedar Cove, but things just haven't been the same
since Max Russell died in our B and B. We still don't have any idea
why he came here and—most important of all—who poisoned him!

But we're not providing the only news in town. I heard that
Maryellen Sherman is getting married and her mother, Grace, has
her pick of interested men—but which one will she choose? And
Olivia Griffin is back from her honeymoon, and her mother, Charlotte,
has a man in her life, too, but I'm not sure Olivia's too pleased....

There's plenty of other gossip I could tell you. Come by for a cup
of tea and one of my blueberry muffins and we'll talk.

44 Cranberry Point

**"Macomber is known for her honest portrayals of
ordinary women in small-town America, and this tale
cements her position as an icon of the genre."**
—*Publishers Weekly* on *16 Lighthouse Road*

*Available the first week of September 2004,
wherever paperbacks are sold.*

www.MIRABooks.com   MDM2073

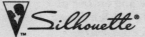

COMING NEXT MONTH